INTERSTELLAR

THE OFFICIAL MOVIE NOVELIZATION

INTERSTELLAR

THE OFFICIAL MOVIE NOVELIZATION

NOVELIZATION BY
GREG KEYES

WRITTEN BY
JONATHAN NOLAN AND
CHRISTOPHER NOLAN

BASED ON THE FILM
FROM WARNER BROS. PICTURES
AND **PARAMOUNT PICTURES**

TITAN BOOKS

INTERSTELLAR
Print edition ISBN: 9781783293698
E-book edition ISBN: 9781783293704

Published by Titan Books
A division of Titan Publishing Group Ltd
144 Southwark Street, London SE1 0UP

First edition: November 2014
10 9

Extract from Dylan Thomas' "Do Not Go Gentle Into That Good Night" taken
from *The Collected Poems of Dylan Thomas: the Centenary Edition* (Orion)
and used with the permission of David Higham Associates on behalf of the
Trustees for the Copyright of Dylan Thomas.

Visit our website: www.titanbooks.com

A CIP catalogue record for this title is available from the British Library.

Printed and bound in the United States.

For Danielle Elizabeth Keyes and Alan Yin.
Best of luck on your own adventure.

INTERSTELLAR

PROLOGUE

First comes darkness, the constant hushed murmur of wind through brittle leaves. And then a woman's voice, quavering pleasantly with age.

"Sure," she says. "Sure, my dad was a farmer back then."

Then the darkness is gone, and all is golden and green as the wind stirs the tassels of waist-high young corn, rattling the stalks as it picks up, as if somewhere a storm is sending notice.

"Like everybody else back then," the woman continues. All at once she is visible against a dark background. The lines of laughter and grief etched into her face, the relief map of a long life.

"Of course," she says, "he didn't start that way."

PART ONE

ONE

The controls jerked in his hands as if they were alive.

Outside the cockpit, white mist streaked by. He could see the nose of his craft, but nothing beyond it.

"*Computer says you're too tight.*" The radio crackled in his ear, the static of shredding ions from the air threatening to overwhelm the signal.

"I got this," he protested, despite the fact that his instruments were telling him impossible things.

"*Crossing the straights,*" control said. "*Shutting it down. Shutting it all down.*"

"No!" he said. "We need to power up—"

He was spinning like crazy now, black and red, black and red, and suddenly the controls ripped free of his hands, and he screamed…

Cooper sat up in the bed, drenched in sweat, and in his mind—still saturated in dream—he was still spinning, still blind in the mist. Panting, he felt the air rushing into and out of his lungs as he tried to control it, to take control of *something*…

"Dad? Dad!"

He turned at the familiar voice, and saw her, in the faint first light of dawn coming through his window. His daughter. The whirlwind of his nightmare faded, and there was only the familiar room, the scent of old wood and mothballs coming from his bedclothes.

"Sorry," he murmured. "Go back to sleep."

She just stood there, though. Murph, as stubborn as ever.

"I thought you were a ghost," she said.

Cooper saw she was serious.

"There's no ghost, Murph," he mumbled.

"Grandpa says you can get ghosts," she persisted.

"Grandpa's a little too close to being one himself," Cooper grunted. "Back to sleep."

Murph still wasn't ready to go. The early morning light picked up the red in her hair, and her green eyes were full of concern. And obstinacy.

"Were you dreaming about the crash?" she asked.

"Back to sleep, Murph," he said, trying to be firm. Murph hesitated, then finally, reluctantly turned and shuffled back through the door.

Rubbing his eyes, Cooper turned to the window. Outside lay a vista of young corn, its leaves dark green, still only waist high. Dawn was painting the tops of the stalks a vivid red-gold. A gentle breeze sent ripples through it, and in his sleep-blurred vision he felt as if he were gazing upon a vast sea, stretching off to the horizon.

TWO

"Corn, sure," the old lady says. "But dust. In your ears, your mouth." We move from her to an old man's face, his watery eyes searching through decades and distance for the road marks left behind him.

"Dust just everywhere," he says, nodding. "Everywhere."

Donald swept the dust from the farmhouse porch, knowing in the back of his mind that it was pointless, that in a matter of hours it would be covered again. Yet simply surrendering to it seemed even more pointless.

This porch—and the sturdy two-story farmhouse to which it was attached—had sheltered generations. It deserved care. Wind and dust had nearly gnawed through the last coat of white paint, and it wasn't likely to get a new coat anytime soon. And it needed bigger repairs than that, work that he was too old to do and Cooper was too busy to see to.

But he could sweep the porch. That much his aging body was still capable of doing. He could beat back the dust, although each assault was a temporary victory at best.

He straightened up and surveyed his work, then loosened the kerchief that stood between the grime and his lungs as he turned and swung open the farmhouse door.

So much for the porch, he thought. It was time to fix breakfast. He made his way to the kitchen, running his fingers through what little bit of thin hair remained on his balding head, feeling the grit matted in it.

Inside, he went to the table, where bowls lay upside down, covered in a thin film of dust, and turned their clean insides up. Then he turned his attention to the stove.

For Donald, the kitchen was probably the most comforting room in the house. His wife had once stood in front of the sturdy enameled ivory oven and stovetop, and in time his daughter had joined her, at first straining on her tiptoes to stir the pot. Then later, as a strong young woman with both feet firmly planted, feeding a family of her own. Both women now gone, but both still here, somehow.

He put the grits on and stirred them as they came to a boil, then turned down the heat so they would simmer, remembering times when breakfast had been a bit more... varied. Oatmeal, waffles, pancakes. Fruit.

Now, mostly grits. And without a lot of the things that made grits worthwhile—the butter, sorghum molasses, bacon for Chrissake. But there wasn't much point in bawling about the things that were gone, was there? And there was plenty good that remained. Time was, a bowl of plain grits was more than most people could hope for in a day. Those days were past, too, and he didn't miss *them* in the slightest.

Count your blessings, old man. He could almost hear the old woman saying it. *No sense moaning 'bout what you can't have.* And by the time the grits were done, counting the better end of his blessings was easy enough—they were all right there in front of him.

There was his grandson Tom, of course. Donald's

grandson was always there when food hit the table. His fifteen-year-old body seemed to travel on two hollow legs. The boy was always hungry—and so he should be, because he was a hard worker, too. He didn't complain about the lack of diversity in breakfast.

Grits were fine with Tom.

His ten-year-old granddaughter Murph was a bit slower to arrive. Her coppery hair was wet, and she still had a towel around her neck from the shower. At times he thought her the spitting image of her mother, but then she would turn in such a way, or say a particular thing, and he could see her father there. Like now. She was fiddling with the pieces of something or other as she sat down. Which she oughtn't to be.

"Not at the table, Murph," he admonished, without any heat in his voice.

But Murph more or less ignored him and looked instead to her father, who had been there all along—before either of his kids—getting his coffee. Cooper was Donald's son-in-law.

He was a good man. He was a decent farmer, too, very much the guy you wanted when you needed a twenty-year-old combine put back in working condition with a handful of wires and an old toaster. Or wanted your solar array to pull in another fifteen percent. He was a whiz with machines. And his daughter had loved him. If he couldn't have his daughter, Cooper was the next best thing, he figured. The man she loved, the children she made.

"Dad, can you fix this?" Murph asked Cooper.

Cooper came over to the table and reached for the pieces of plastic she had pinched between her fingertips, a frown presenting on his lean face. Donald saw now what it was—the broken model of an Apollo lunar lander.

"What'd you do to my lander?" Cooper asked.

"Wasn't me," Murph said.

"Lemme guess," Tom sneered, through a mouthful of grits. "Your ghost?"

Murph appeared not to hear Tom. She had lately seemed to discover that ignoring him irritated him far more than any rejoinder she might come up with.

"It knocked it off my shelf," she said to her father, quite matter-of-factly. "It keeps knocking books off."

"There's no such thing as ghosts, dumb-ass," Tom said.

"Hey!" Cooper said, sending him a hard look. Tom just shrugged and looked unrepentant.

But Murph wouldn't let go.

"I looked it up," she said. "It's called a poltergeist."

"Dad, tell her," Tom pleaded.

"Murph," Cooper said, "you know that's not scientific." But his daughter stared at him stubbornly.

"You say science is about admitting what we *don't* know," she said.

"She's got you there," Donald said.

Cooper handed Murph back the pieces.

"Start looking after our stuff," he said.

Donald caught Cooper's eye.

"Coop," he admonished.

Cooper shrugged. Donald was right. Murph was smart, but she needed a little guidance.

"Fine," he said. "Murph, you wanna talk science, don't just tell me you're scared of some ghost. Record the facts, analyze — present your conclusions."

"Sure," Murph said, and her expression said that the wheels were turning already.

Cooper seemed to think that settled things. He grabbed his keys and stood up.

"Hold up," Donald said. "Parent–teacher conferences. Parent... not grandparent."

* ❊ *

Donald meant well, but Cooper was still feeling the sting of his comment as the kids climbed into the battered old pickup truck, knocking the night's layer of dust off of the seats. The old pickup showed almost as much rust as it did the original blue paint job, and enough dents and scratches to prove what a workhorse it had been.

Sure, he'd missed a few of these school things, now and then—he was busy. He was a single father. Was it so bad to ask Donald to pick up a little of the slack? It wasn't like Cooper didn't spend time with the kids. Quality time.

But that didn't mean jumping through whatever hoops the school demanded of him. He had better things to do.

As he opened the driver's-side door, he took another sip of his coffee, peering at the black cloud rising in the distance, trying to gauge it, estimate how far away it was. Whose fields were there? Which way was it moving?

"Dust storm?" he wondered aloud.

Donald shook his head.

"Nelson's torching his whole crop."

"Blight?" Cooper asked.

"They're saying it's the last harvest for okra," Donald replied. "Ever."

Cooper watched the black smoke, wondering if that could be right, knowing in the pit of his gut it probably was. But what good was okra, anyway? Slimy stuff, unless you fried it. Used to thicken soup. A luxury, not a staple. It was an insignificant loss.

"Shoulda planted corn like the rest of us," he said as he got into the truck. Nelson had always had more nerve than sense.

"Be nice to Miss Hanley," Donald said. "She's single."

"What's that supposed to mean?" Cooper snapped, knowing full well what the old man was getting at.

"Repopulating the Earth," Donald clarified. "Start pulling your weight."

He seemed to get nosier every day. Cooper wasn't sure where the line was, but he thought the old man had crossed it a while back, and was now just sort of camping out smack in the middle of his private concerns.

"Start minding your business," Cooper shot back. But he knew the old man meant well.

Moments later they were wheeling down the dirt road. Cooper gripped the steering wheel with one hand and his coffee with the other. Murph was sandwiched between him and Tom.

"Okay," he said to her as first gear began to wind out. He stepped on the clutch. "Gimme second."

Murph wrestled the long shifter into second gear as Cooper took another sip of coffee and let the pedal up.

"Now third," he said after a few seconds, as the truck picked up speed. He pushed down again, and Murph struggled with the stick. He heard the transmission grind in protest as she failed to locate third.

"Find a gear, dumb-ass," Tom rebuked.

"Shut up, Tom!" Cooper scolded his son.

His reprimand was punctuated by a loud *bang*, followed by an abrupt roughening of the ride.

"What'd you do, Murph?" Tom demanded.

"She didn't do anything," Cooper said. "We lost a tire, is all." He pulled over—not that anyone was likely to come along.

"Murphy's Law," Tom said, a little too gleefully. He made a little "ouch!" face at her.

"Shut up, Tom," Murph said, and she shot him a withering look.

Cooper pushed open the door, climbed out, looked at the tire, and saw that yeah, it was pretty damn flat. He turned to Tom.

"Grab the spare," he said.

"That *is* the spare," Tom replied, opening his door and joining his father.

"Okay," Cooper said. "Patch kit."

"How am I supposed to patch it out here?" Tom protested.

"Figure it out," he told his son. "I'm not always going to be here to help you." Then he went around the back and to the other side of the truck. He found Murph leaning there, still fuming a little.

"Why'd you and Mom name me after something bad?" she demanded.

"We didn't," he told her.

"Murphy's Law?" she asked, equal parts dubious and indignant.

Cooper studied his daughter's earnest expression. He remembered the young man and woman who had named her.

"Murphy's Law doesn't mean bad stuff will happen," he explained gently, really wanting her to understand. "It means 'whatever can happen... will happen.' And that sounded just fine to us."

Murph frowned, and at first he thought she was about to protest further, but then he realized she wasn't really paying attention to him anymore. Her eyes were far away, as if she had suddenly turned into a frequency he couldn't receive.

"What?" he asked. But then he heard it too, a long, low rumble, rising in pitch due to the Doppler effect. Something was coming toward them—no, *flying* toward them—and he was sure he recognized the noise it was making. But it had been so long, it was a little hard to believe his ears.

He grabbed Murph and pushed her back toward her seat in the truck, just as a projectile blew past overhead—a missile-shaped object with long, narrow, tapered wings jutting out at right angles.

"Come on!" he shouted. He leapt into the truck, fumbling for the laptop computer and the antenna that was connected to it. He quickly passed them to Murph, then yelled at Tom, who had the jack in his hand and was looking up from the flat tire.

"Get in!"

"What about the tire?" the boy asked.

But there was no time to worry about that now.

THREE

The drone could not, of course, be bothered to follow roads, so neither could they. As fast as the truck would go, they were tearing through a cornfield, flattening the stalks beneath three tires and a wobbling rim.

He tried not to think about how much of the crop he was destroying, but at least it was his own field. He wouldn't have an angry lynch mob showing up at the house in a few hours. And he knew it was justified. The corn was precious, yes, but you didn't see one of these things every day.

Or month.

Or… year.

Cooper darted his gaze about frantically, trying to see through the corn, over it, but between the high stalks and the roof of the truck there was only a narrow window of visibility.

Across the cab, scrunched against the passenger-side door, Murph had the laptop booted up. Tom was in the middle this time, and Coop was doing his own shifting.

"There!" Tom shouted, pointing off to the right. Cooper ducked his head and looked up.

And there it was, only meters above the corn.

What the hell is it doing? he thought. *What's it searching for?* Cooper spun the wheel, fishtailing them toward the thing that looked like a small plane without a cockpit.

Then he recognized the silhouette.

"Indian air force surveillance drone," Cooper said. "Solar cells could power an entire farm."

He glanced at Tom.

"Take the wheel," he said.

After a quick display of mutual contortion, Tom was in the driver's seat and Cooper was in the middle with the laptop. He handed Murph the antenna.

"Keep it pointed right at it," he told her. Then he went to work on the computer. After a moment the screen began to fill with the flowing, almost liquid lines of the Devanagari script. But success gave way to disappointment—the signal was dropping away.

"Faster, Tom," he said. "I'm losing it."

Tom took the command to heart, flooring the pedal of the old truck and zigzagging through the corn with abandon. The signal jumped back up, and Cooper kept working at the encryption. The truck burst from the corn and onto open ground.

"Dad?" Tom said.

"Almost got it," he told his son, eyes locked on the screen. "Don't stop."

The drone vanished from view, dropping over the horizon. They must be close to the next valley, Cooper figured, for it to be able to pull that trick.

"*Dad…*" Tom said, his voice sounding a little more urgent.

Cooper looked up, just in time to see they were barreling toward the sharp drop into the reservoir. His eyes went wide, and his heart dropped into his shoes.

"Tom!" he yelped.

The boy slammed on the brakes. Rocks pinged off the

bottom of the truck, and they skidded to a halt in a cloud of dust, dangerously near the drop. Breathing heavily, Cooper stared for a moment, thinking how it was good they hadn't had four working tires, because they would have been going even faster…

He looked over at Tom.

His son just shrugged.

"You told me to keep going," he said.

Heart still racing, Cooper reached past his daughter and pushed open the passenger door. Murph hopped out the truck and he followed, laptop in hand.

"Guess that answers the 'if I told you to drive off a cliff' scenario," he muttered, mostly to himself. Then he looked at Murph to make sure she was okay. She still had the antenna pointed hopefully beyond the bluff.

"We lost it," she said.

Her disappointment made the grin Cooper felt tugging at his lips feel all the better.

"No, we didn't," he said, as the drone came soaring back over them. He continued piloting it with the track pad, banking it in a broad arc above. Both kids watched the machine, a marvel from another era, as it dipped and straightened its wings at his command. Tom looked mildly excited. Murph was clearly in awe.

"Want to give it a whirl?" he asked Murph.

He didn't have to ask twice. As he guided her fingers across the pad, her face lit up with amazement and joy. It was wonderful to see, and he wanted to stretch the moment out forever.

But they had things to do.

"Let's set her down next to the reservoir," he said, after a bit.

Spotting a wide, flat spot, Cooper brought the drone to the ground. Then they drove, slowly and unsteadily, across the rough ground, rocks and gravel scraping against the wheel that sported only tattered fragments of the ruined tire.

The drone was almost as long as the truck, but slim and tubular.

What a beauty, he thought, rubbing his palm across the smooth, dark surface, imagining the clever hands that had built it, feeling almost like a kid again himself. Not that long ago, mankind had made such marvelous, beautiful things.

"How long you think it's been up there?" Tom asked.

"Delhi mission control went down same as ours, ten years ago," Cooper answered.

"It's been up there ten years?" Tom said, his tone incredulous. "Why'd it come down so low?"

"Sun finally cooked its brain," Cooper speculated. "Or it came down looking for something."

"What?" Murph wanted to know.

"Some kind of signal," he replied. He shook his head. "Who knows?"

Cooper explored the surface of the machine until he found the access panel. Other than his own efforts—and the faint, sluggish movement of the river—all was still. A slight breeze mingled the scent of burnt corn with aquatic decay. Like everything else, the reservoir had known better days.

He pried open the panel and peered into the box that housed the drone's brain.

"What are you going to do with it?" Murph asked.

"Give it something scientifically responsible to do," Cooper said. "Like drive a combine." He moved to one end and hefted it experimentally. He and Tom would be able to get it into the truck.

"Couldn't we just let it go?" she asked. "It's not hurting anyone."

Cooper glanced down fondly at his daughter. She had a good heart, and generous sensibilities. And a part of him ached at the thought of taking this thing that had roamed freely on the winds for more than a decade—maybe the last of its kind, one of the last flying machines ever—and enslaving it to a field of corn. But unlike Murph, he knew that such feelings had to come second to the necessity.

"This thing has to adapt," he explained. "Just like the rest of us."

By the time they finally limped up to the school, the sleek drone hanging out of the back of the battered truck, Cooper was fighting down a certain amount of anxiety about the parent–teacher conferences.

"How's this work?" he asked tentatively. "You guys come with?"

"I've got class," Tom informed him with a hint of superiority. Then he patted Murph on the shoulder. "But *she* needs to wait."

Murph sent Tom another venom-filled glare as he nimbly exited the vehicle.

"Why?" Cooper asked. "What?" As his son disappeared toward the door, he turned to his daughter.

Murph looked uncomfortable as she scribbled something in her notebook.

"Dad," she began, "I had a… thing. Well, they'll tell you about it. Just try and…"

"Am I gonna be mad?" Cooper demanded, raising his eyebrows.

"Not with me," Murph said. "Just try not to…"

"Relax," he reassured her. "I got this."

FOUR

Cooper hadn't cared for the principal's office when he was a boy. Now he found he cared for it even less. He felt nervous and jittery—almost as if *he* had done something wrong.

The principal—William Okafor—was looking out of his window as Cooper stepped in, and he turned to greet his visitor. He was a bit younger than Cooper himself. The authority that was so casually attached to him seemed outsized for the job of riding herd on less than a hundred students. His dark suit and black tie only enhanced the impression, and made Cooper more nervous.

What would he have been thirty years ago? A corporate executive? A military officer? The president of a university?

There was a woman in the room, as well, and he nodded to her. She nodded back. He wondered if she was Miss Hanley, and remembered Donald's advice to be nice to her. He had to admit that she wasn't too hard on the eyes. Long blonde hair braided and tied around the top of her head. Conservative skirt and light blue sweater.

"Little late, Coop," Okafor chastised. He pointed at the empty chair in front of his desk and then nodded out the window toward Cooper's truck.

"Ah… we had a flat," Cooper said.

"And I guess you had to stop off at the Asian fighter-plane store." He sounded a combination of disapproving and curious.

Cooper sat, trying to smile.

"Actually, sir, it's a surveillance drone," he explained. "With outstanding solar cells."

The principal didn't seem impressed, and he picked up a piece of paper, scanning it.

"We got Tom's scores back," he said. "He's going to make an excellent farmer." He pushed a paper across his desk. "Congratulations."

Cooper glanced at it.

"Yeah, he's got the knack for it," he conceded.

But Tom could do better.

"What about college?" he asked.

"The university only takes a handful," Okafor replied. "They don't have the resources—"

That was too much for Cooper.

"I'm still paying taxes," he erupted indignantly. "Where's that go? There's no more armies…"

The principal shook his head slowly.

"Not to the university, Coop," he said. "You have to be realistic."

Realistic? Cooper only felt his outrage growing. This was his *kid*. *This* was Tom.

"You're ruling him out *now*?" Cooper persisted, not willing to let go. "He's fifteen."

"Tom's score simply isn't high enough," Okafor replied.

Trying to keep it together, Cooper pointed at the principal's pants.

"What're you?" he demanded. "About a 36-inch waist?"

Okafor just stared at him, clearly unsure where he was going with this.

"Thirty-inch inseam?" Cooper added.

Okafor continued to look at him without comprehension.

"I'm not sure I see what—" he began with a little frown.

"You're telling me," Cooper plowed on, "you need two numbers to measure your own ass, but just one to measure my son's future?"

Miss Hanley stifled a laugh. So she had a sense of humor, too. That was okay. But she looked rebuffed when the principal shot her a nasty look before putting his game face back on.

"You're a well-educated man, Coop," he said, trying to regain the upper hand. "A trained pilot—"

"And an engineer," Cooper put in, not willing to be shortchanged by this condescending pri… principal.

"Okay," Okafor said, leaning forward. "Well, right now the world doesn't need more engineers. We didn't run out of planes, or television sets. We ran out of *food*."

Cooper sat back in the chair, feeling the steam leak out of him.

"The world needs farmers," Okafor continued, with a smile that was probably meant to be benign but just felt patronizing. "Good farmers, like you. And Tom. We're a caretaker generation. And things are getting better. Maybe your grandchildren—"

Cooper suddenly just wanted to be very far from this man, this conversation, this situation—all of it.

"Are we done, sir?" he asked abruptly.

But it wasn't going to be that easy. Nothing ever was.

"No," the principal said. "Miss Hanley is here to talk about Murph."

Reluctantly, Cooper shifted his gaze to Miss Hanley. What was coming next? Were they going to tell him that Murph wasn't sixth-grade material? Because if that was the case, there were some modifications he could make to his combines.

They could make a real mess of this place.

"Murph's a bright kid," she began, dispelling that worry, but raining a metric ton of others. "A wonderful kid, Mr. Cooper. But she's been having a little trouble…"

Here we go, Cooper thought. *The "but."*

Miss Hanley placed a textbook on the desk.

"She brought this to school," she said. "To show the other kids the section on lunar landings…"

"Yeah," he said, recognizing it. "It's one of my old textbooks. She likes the pictures."

"This is an old federal textbook," Miss Hanley said. "We've replaced them with corrected versions."

"Corrected?" Cooper asked.

"Explaining how the Apollo missions were faked to bankrupt the Soviet Union."

He was so stunned that for a moment he wasn't sure how he was supposed to react.

Laugh? Cry?

Explode?

He settled for incredulity.

"You don't believe we went to the moon?" Sure, he was aware that there had always been a fringe element—crazies who held to that cock-eyed nonsense. But a teacher? How could anyone with half a mind peddle that baloney?

She smiled at him as if he were a three-year-old.

"I believe it was a brilliant piece of propaganda," she allowed. "The Soviets bankrupted themselves pouring resources into rockets and other useless machines."

"Useless machines?" Cooper asked, feeling his fuse grow shorter.

Of course, she kept going.

"Yes, Mr. Cooper," she said, tolerantly. "And if we don't want to repeat the wastefulness of the twentieth century, our children need to learn about *this* planet. Not tales of leaving it."

Cooper tried to absorb that for a moment. His fuse was still burning, flaring even, sputtering toward the keg.

"One of those useless machines they used to make," he finally began, "was called an MRI. And if we had any of them left, the doctors would have been able to find the cyst in my wife's brain *before* she died, rather than afterwards. Then *she* would be sitting here listening to this, which'd be good, 'cos she was always the calmer one…"

Miss Hanley looked first confused, then embarrassed, then a little aghast, but before she could say anything, Okafor broke in.

"I'm sorry about your wife, Mr. Cooper," he said. "But Murph got into a fistfight with several of her classmates over this Apollo nonsense, and we thought it best to bring you in and see what ideas you might have for dealing with her behavior on the home front." With that, he stopped and waited.

Cooper regarded the two of them for a moment, thinking how unreal it was, how everything seemed sort of normal sometimes, and then you realized how upside down things had actually turned.

Am I that out of touch? he wondered. *Has it really gotten that bad?*

He guessed he was, and that it had. He didn't pay much attention to what little news there was, because he had long ago realized it was really mostly propaganda. But he hadn't realized they had gone so far as to rewrite the freaking *textbooks*.

Principal Okafor and Miss Hanley were waiting expectantly. They wanted to know how he was going to punish Murph for her temerity. How he was going to straighten her out.

They deserved an answer.

"Sure," he said, finally, carefully measuring out his words. "Well, there's a ball game tomorrow night, and Murph's going through a bit of a baseball phase. There'll be candy and soda…"

A look of approval had begun to appear on Miss Hanley's face. He remembered Donald's words again. But even if he were anywhere near to being in the market for another wife, no amount of looks could make up for this amount of stupid. He regarded her bluntly.

"I think I'll take her to that," he told her.

She blinked as if she didn't understand, then turned to Okafor, a very unhappy expression starting upon her pretty features.

The principal didn't look so happy himself.

"How'd it go?" Murph asked a few minutes later, as he approached the pickup.

"I, uh… got you suspended," he admitted.

"What?" she gasped.

"Sorry," he muttered.

"Dad!" she said, her voice rising. "I told you not to—"

The CB radio in the truck suddenly squawked to life.

"*Cooper?*" it crackled. "*Boots for Cooper.*"

With a certain amount of relief, he brushed past his distressed daughter and picked up the handset, holding it close alongside his mouth.

"Cooper," he replied.

"*Coop, those combines you rebuilt went haywire,*" Boots asserted. He sounded a little excited, which was unusual. Boots had been Cooper's chief farmhand for half a decade, but he'd been farming since childhood, and had pretty much seen it all.

"Power the controllers down for a few minutes," Cooper said, still aware of Murph's expression of disbelief, and trying to avoid catching her eye.

"*Did that,*" Boots replied. "*You should come take a look, it's kinda weird.*"

FIVE

Kinda weird? Cooper thought as they passed the enormous boxy harvester that was pulling up to the house. *How about, "Freakin' weird?"*

The harvester wasn't alone. Dozens of automated farming machines had arrived in his front yard and stopped, nudged up to his porch as if they were waiting to be let in. It reminded Cooper of a nativity scene, with the machines playing the parts of the animals.

As he and Murph got out of the truck to more fully appreciate the bizarre tableau, Boots arrived. His white hair marked him as a bit older than Cooper. He was no great thinker, but he knew farming as well as anyone.

"One by one they been peeling off from the fields and heading over," Boots said.

Cooper walked over to the harvester, opened up the cabin, and had a look at the autopilot that worked the controls.

"Something's interfering with their compass," Boots went on. "Magnetism or some such…"

That much was obvious, Cooper thought. But what was there in the house that could exert that sort of magnetic force? He thought about the drone, which also had been called by something unknown—if not to his house, then at least to the same general area. What were the odds of both things happening in the same day?

They seemed pretty low.

He wheeled and strode toward the house, not at all sure what he was looking for. Whatever it was, though, he was damned determined that he was gonna find it.

He didn't see anything in the kitchen, though. Murph walked in behind him.

"What is it, Dad?"

Before he could answer, there was a pronounced— if not particularly loud—*thump* from upstairs. Cooper moved quickly to the stairs, then climbed them warily, all sorts of thoughts scurrying through his mind.

Maybe someone else had been trying to hijack the drone, and now they were screwing with his machines, invading his house?

Maybe it was something else—another drone, crashed into the upstairs, calling desperately for its winged comrade in some command code that was affecting the farm equipment.

He was certain now, in his mind, that it couldn't have been a coincidence—the drone, the way the harvesters were acting. There had to be a connection.

Damned if I can figure out what it can be, though... He hesitated slightly at the threshold to Murph's bedroom. The door was open, and he could see inside.

One entire wall was a bookshelf, floor to ceiling. Most of the books they contained had once belonged to his wife, Erin, just as the room itself had been hers when she was a girl. Long before they had married.

Now it was Murph's room.

He noticed there were now gaps in what had once been overstuffed bookshelves. The missing books were on the floor. Suddenly he remembered Murph's comments, earlier in the day.

"Nothing special about *which* books," Murph said, moving into the room from behind him. "Been working on it, like you said." She held up the notebook in which she'd been drawing. The page was covered by a pattern that looked something like a barcode.

"I counted the spaces," she said, as if that explained it all.

"Why?" Cooper asked.

"In case the ghost is trying to say something," she explained. "I'm trying Morse."

"Morse?" he said.

"Yeah, dots and dashes, used for—"

"Murph," he said, trying to be gentle. "I know what Morse code is. I just don't think your bookshelf's trying to talk to you."

She looked at him with a mixture of hurt and embarrassment. But she didn't even try to reply.

Donald offered him a beer. Cooper took it, and gazed aimlessly off toward the dark fields, the old man sitting there beside him in a chair that was probably as old as he was.

"Had to reset every compass clock and GPS to offset for the anomaly," Cooper said.

"Which is?" Donald asked.

Cooper took a swig of the beer. It was cold, and it felt good in his throat, but for him it would never quite taste right. Beer was supposed to be made of barley. Not corn. But barley was sleeping with the dinosaurs now, courtesy of the blight.

"No idea," he said, finally admitting that for all of his

apparently outdated training and knowledge, he didn't have an explanation any more scientific than his daughter's ghost. "If the house was built on magnetic ore, we'd've seen this the first time we switched on a tractor."

Donald nodded and sipped his own drink. He didn't press it any further. Instead he changed to an even less pleasant subject.

"Sounds like your meeting at school didn't go so well."

Cooper sighed, thinking back to the encounter, trying to pinpoint exactly what it was that had left him feeling so angry. Was it the lie about Apollo?

Partly. But that was just part of something bigger.

"We've forgotten who we are, Donald," he said. "Explorers. Pioneers. Not *caretakers*."

Donald nodded thoughtfully. Cooper waited, knowing Donald would take his time if he thought he had something important to say—weigh up his words like kilos of corn before broadcasting the least of them.

"When I was a kid," he finally said, "it felt like they made something new every day. Some gadget or idea. Like every day was Christmas. But *six billion people*…" He shook his head. "Just try to imagine that. And every last one of them trying to have it all." He shifted to face Cooper directly. "This world isn't so bad. Tom'll do just fine—you're the one who doesn't belong. Born forty years too late, and forty years too early. My daughter knew it, God bless her. And your kids know it.

"'Specially Murph," he added.

Cooper turned his gaze skyward, where the stars were showing them something that didn't happen that much anymore. A show worth staying up for. He could pick out the Seven Sisters and Orion's belt and the dim, faintly red orb of Mars. Humanity had been headed there, once. *He* had been headed there, or at least that had been the general idea.

"We used to look up and wonder at our place in the stars," he said. "Now we just look down and worry about our place in the dirt."

Donald's expression was sympathetic.

"Cooper," he said, "you were good at something, and you never got a chance to do anything with it. I'm sorry. But that's not your kids' fault."

Cooper knew he didn't have anything to say to that, so he didn't even try. He just continued watching the slow wheel of the night sky, the thousands of stars he could see, the trillions he couldn't due to atmosphere and distance. Men and women had been out there. Men had gone to the moon, and no rewriting of any textbook would ever change that reality.

No matter how inconvenient a fact it might be for the *caretakers*.

SIX

Something in the face of the old man shifts. His eyes are looking at something we cannot see. Should not see.

"May 14th," he says. "Never forget. Clear as a bell. You'd never think…"

Another man's face, also old, and his expression is close kin to that of the first.

"When the first of the real big ones rolled in," he says, "I thought it was the end of the world."

The crack of the bat brought Cooper's wandering mind back to the game, at least for a moment.

He watched the ball shoot up, like a rocket determined to break through the stratosphere, only to slow, briefly stop, and arc sharply back down to the mitt waiting to catch it. He gazed around at the half-filled stands, where a smattering of applause didn't seem to really add up to enthusiasm.

"In my day we had real ball players," Donald complained. "Who're these bums?"

The pop fly was the third out, and the team on the field started in—"New York Yankees" printed plainly on their uniforms.

"Well, in *my* day people were too busy fighting over food for baseball," Cooper reminded him, "so consider this progress."

Murph reached a bag of popcorn toward Donald.

"Fine," the old man grumbled, looking at the bag as if it might contain manure. "But popcorn at a ball game is unnatural. I want a hot dog."

Cooper watched his daughter's face frame her confusion.

"What's a hot dog?" she asked.

Cooper glanced at Tom, sitting next to him. They hadn't spoken since his conversation with the principal, but it was probably time to address it. So after a moment, with some hesitation, he put his arm around the boy.

"The school says you're gonna follow in my footsteps," he told the boy. "I think that's great."

Tom offered him a skeptical look.

"You think that's great?" he said.

"You *hate* farming, Dad," Murph piped up. "Grandpa said."

Not helping here… Cooper sent a frown back toward Donald, who just lifted his shoulders in a half-assed apology. *Not helping at all.*

Feeling a little of the wind go out of him, Cooper turned his attention back to Tom.

"What's important is how *you* feel about it, Tom," he said. The boy was silent for a moment, as he thought about it.

"I like what you do," Tom said. He wasn't joking, or trying to be ironic, but answering sincerely. "I like our farm."

Cooper heard the bat crack again, but this time the crowd didn't respond at all. In fact, the players on the field didn't either—no one was running bases or trying to catch the ball. Instead, one by one, their gazes were turning upward.

Cooper looked up, as well.

* ✳ *

"You've never seen the like," the old man says, his voice thick with remembered fear. "Black. Just black."

The storm was building itself on the horizon, a wall of dust churning toward them. Cooper always thought they looked more like tsunamis than storms, and this one more than most. The air was sharp with ozone, and already the wind was picking up as the dry, cold front that drove the storm shoved the warm evening air before it and away.

The temperature had already dropped a few degrees. The hairs on his arms stood, as crooked lines of blue-white fire danced in the Stygian tempest like the demons of some ancient mythology, come to demand sacrifice.

Maybe that's next, Cooper thought. Burnt offerings to appease the dust, to ease the blight. Why stop at rejecting the last century-and-a-half of scientific achievement? Why not claw it all the way back to Babylon and Sumer?

The game was over, that much was sure. Already people were streaming from the stadium, kerchiefs over their faces ready for when the dust hit.

So much for the family evening out.

"Come on, guys," Cooper said.

Cooper had hoped to outrun the dust storm at first, but that hope was dimming along with the light from the sun. Donald and the kids were frantically stuffing rags into vents, cracks, and anyplace the insidious dust might enter the truck.

He knew from experience it wouldn't be enough.

Through the rearview mirror he saw the monster

advancing, watched buildings and roads vanish into it. The truck was beginning to jerk and rock.

Then the wall hit them, and everything went dark. The wheel tried to wrench itself out of his hands as Cooper fought desperately to stay on the road—if he was even still on it. He couldn't see more than a yard past his windshield, and the pavement was so cracked and eroded, it felt scarcely different from open ground under his tires. It would be easy to stray. Like Jansen, who had driven right into an old stream bed and been buried in a drift. Of course, Jansen never had much of a sense of direction in the best of times.

"It's a bad one," Donald noticed.

No shit, Cooper thought. The storm that had buried Jansen hadn't been half as bad as this one. There couldn't really be any doubt that they were getting worse as the years went on. Mother Nature reasserting her superiority with ever-increasing enthusiasm.

"Mask up, guys," Cooper said. Murph and Tom both obeyed immediately, pulling surgical masks out of the glove compartment and fitting them onto their faces.

The truck shuddered as the storm moaned around them. Cooper navigated through the brief breaks in the darkness. Visibility could be measured in feet, and on two hands. Wind belted the truck, again and again.

Cooper's one advantage was that the land around his place was pretty flat—no hills to pull, no downslopes. If he felt anything like that, it would mean he was way off target, and he would know instantly to slam on the brakes and wait it out.

In the end, it was mostly muscle memory that got them home. He'd made the trip from town so often that the distance and turns were furrowed into his brain. As they crept up to the farm, he finally had time to worry beyond the moment, to wonder what the damage would be this time, how many solar panels would need replacing, how many windows had been shattered. How much of the crop he was going to find flattened.

How long it would take to get the freaking dust off the floor, out of their bedclothes, cups, saucers, pitchers...

Underwear.

He peered out to get a better look, the house coming and going from vision in the black blizzard.

He jerked back as a sheet of metal slammed into the windshield. They waited a few moments to recover from the surprise, then Donald opened the passenger door, took Tom's arm and the two of them started slogging, eyes closed, toward the house.

Cooper took hold of Murph and dragged her out of the vehicle.

Even with his eyes closed, the dust got in, and even with a mask on, some of it got to his lungs. And it was easy to get lost in one of these storms, even when you knew you were just a few feet away from safety—or at least protection from the wind that made projectiles out of everything not nailed down. Shielding Murph with his body, he pushed toward the house. Then he came up against the porch, put wood under his feet, and followed Donald and Tom through the front door.

It wasn't, after all, his first storm.

Inside, shutters banged, dust jetted up through cracks in the floorboards and windowsills, and it rolled in through the front door in huge gusts until Donald slammed it shut behind them.

Cooper darted his gaze about, surveying the damage, and suddenly noticed a dark cloud rolling down the stairs.

Cooper looked at his kids.

"Did you both shut your windows?" he demanded. Tom nodded yes, but the expression on Murph's face told him what he already knew. In a flash she was running up the stairs, hurrying to amend her mistake.

"Wait!" he cried, following her.

When he got to her room she was just standing there, staring at the floor, with the window still wide open. The rush and howl of the storm were fighting their way into the room. Suppressing some inelegant turns of phrase, he crossed the floor, gripped the wooden frame, and slammed it shut, instantly distancing the sounds.

Bereft of wind, the dust hung in the air, as fine and insidious as powdered graphite.

Murph just stood there, gawking at the floor, her eyes wide as dinner plates. And then Cooper saw why. Streaks were forming in the suspended dust, as if a giant invisible comb was being pulled through the air from floor to ceiling. Then he realized the dust was actually streaming down with unnatural speed, collecting on the floor; not randomly, but into lines—lines that formed into a distinguishable pattern.

"The ghost," Murph said.

The ghost. Cooper didn't bother to contradict her this time. He was too busy staring himself.

The dust was collecting as if it were falling on wires, but there were no wires to see. He was reminded of a very old toy which had been his uncle's when he was a boy. Basically it consisted of a piece of cardboard with a human face drawn on it, covered by a flat plastic bubble. There were finely cut iron filings inside of the bubble. The toy came with a pencil-shaped magnet, and if you held the magnet behind the cardboard, you could drag the filings around to form hair and a beard on the face.

From the front it appeared as if an unseen force was dragging the filings into shape. Which of course was the case, since a magnetic field is invisible to the human eye. Yet the source of that little trick—the magnetic field—the magnet—could easily be discovered by any observer who looked behind the cardboard.

Not so, what was happening before his eyes.

Dust wasn't metal. It wasn't attracted by magnetic fields. And below the pattern there was only floor; no hand—human or otherwise—was wielding a hidden magnet. Yet undeniably, something was attracting the dust, and not randomly.

Someone was behind the cardboard with... something.

He felt a little prickle on the back of his spine. The drone. The harvesters.

Now this.

"Grab your pillow," he told Murph. "Sleep in with Tom."

She went, but with considerable hesitation.

SEVEN

Murph woke the next morning, trying to figure out what was wrong. Where she was. She certainly wasn't in her room, but in a far smellier place.

Then the pile of covers on the bed snorted and she got it—she was in Tom's room, for some reason.

Then she remembered it all. The dust storm, the open window, the ghost tracing lines with the dust. Trying to go to sleep, wanting desperately to see what the ghost had drawn. Then finally sleep, and crazier dreams than she usually had.

Now, at last, morning had come.

It was cold, so she wrapped herself in a blanket before leaving Tom's room and padding down the hall to her own, worried there wouldn't be anything—just a pile of dust. Just another thing for her dad to dismiss as nothing. As her imagination.

He was always ready to get into a fight when other people didn't take her seriously—like at the school yesterday. But when it came down to it, he was the worst one of all.

So she went on to her room, braced for disappointment.

But when she walked quietly through the doorway, her dad was there already, and she realized with a shock that he might have been there all night.

The dust had settled now, leaving a thin mantel throughout the house, on everything. It all would need cleaning soon.

Except here, in her room.

Her dad was staring at a pattern of lines in the dust— some thick, some thinner. It reminded her of her drawing from the day before.

Murph sat down next to her dad. He didn't say anything at first—just held up a coin.

"It's not a ghost," he said.

Then he tossed the coin across the pattern. The second it crossed a line, it turned and shot straight down to the floor.

"It's gravity."

Donald wearily traversed the stairs, where he found Cooper and Murph in Erin's... Murph's room, still studying the dust on the floor. They had been there all morning— probably all night, as well.

Neither of them looked up when he came in.

"I'm dropping Tom," Donald informed him, "then heading to town." He glanced down at the pattern on the floor, at the little science-fair project with which Cooper and Murph were both obsessed.

"You wanna clean that up when you've finished praying to it?" he gruffed.

No answer.

All right then...

As he left, Cooper wordlessly took Murph's notebook from her hands and started scribbling in it.

* ✵ *

After Grandpa and Tom left, Murph spent a lot of time thinking about her ghost, and what it was trying to tell her.

She was glad Dad was finally paying attention to the strange things that had been happening in her room, but in a way she was starting to feel a little vexed. This was *her* investigation, wasn't it? He had told her that himself, challenged her to make it all scientific. Well, she'd taken him at his word, and still he hadn't taken her seriously.

Now, when *he* saw something weird, he was all over it. With *her* notebook.

At some point her belly began to growl, so she went downstairs and made sandwiches. She poured two glasses of water and took it all up to her room. Dad was probably hungry, too, since he hadn't had breakfast.

This time when she came in, he looked up at her.

"I got something," he said, pointing to the thick and thin lines. "Binary. Thick is one, thin is zero."

He was excited, she could tell. Maybe more excited than she had ever seen him. His eyes were bright and a little grin hung on his face. He held up her notebook and showed her pairs of numbers he had scribbled there.

"Coordinates," he said.

A few minutes later, he had pulled a bunch of maps from a closet and had spread them on the kitchen table. He extracted a couple from the stack and tossed them aside, then tapped one and spread it out fully, tracing his finger across the contours, crossing the blue squiggles of streams that were now dry beds, past the names of towns where empty buildings crumbled gradually into the soil and dust.

He wondered if there would ever be any new maps. Maybe. But not like this one, informed by satellites and flyovers. No, the next maps would be made with tape measures and alidades, by men and women carrying machetes to clear the brush.

If they were lucky. If surveying even survived the "revised" textbooks.

His finger settled on the spot where the prescribed longitude and latitude met. There was nothing marked on the map, but he hadn't expected there to be.

Time for a road trip, he thought eagerly.

EIGHT

Murph watched Cooper with an unhappy expression on her face as he stuffed sleeping bag, flashlight, and other supplies into the truck.

"You can't leave me behind!" she protested again.

"Grandpa's back in two hours," he told her. But he knew that wasn't what she meant.

"You don't know what you're going to find!" she said.

"That's why I can't take you," he said. What wasn't she getting? Why couldn't she understand? When gravity writes map directions on the floor of your house, you don't take your little girl to find out how and why. He wasn't an idiot.

She blinked at him angrily, and then ran back toward the house.

So she'll be mad at me for a while, he figured. *I'll find a way to make it up to her.* It was better than putting her at risk.

A few minutes later, satisfied with his loading, Cooper went back into the house for the maps and some bottled water. He hesitated a moment, looking up the stairs to where Murph was probably sulking in her room.

"Murph!" he called, but she didn't answer. Which wasn't surprising. He wondered if he should go up and talk to her, but he felt like it would just be a waste of time.

"Murph, just wait here for Grandpa," he yelled up. "Tell him I'll call him on the radio."

Then he went back through the door, climbed into his truck, and headed out.

Toward what? His daughter had a gravitational anomaly in her bedroom. Well, there were gravitational anomalies all around the world—plenty of them if you weren't too picky by what you meant. Gravity and mass were intimately linked—the more massive something was, the more it bent space-time, the more it attracted other bodies.

But anomalies didn't tend to pop up in the course of a day, in a tiny spot in someone's house, someone's *bedroom*. And they didn't usually present patterns that turned out to be map coordinates, translated into binary code. Coordinates to a place that was relatively nearby.

He spread the map across the steering wheel and looked around for a pen. There wasn't one in the passenger seat, or the glove compartment, so he reached down to the passenger-side leg space, where a blanket covered a clutter of stuff. He lifted up the blanket.

A grinning face suddenly appeared, framed in red hair.

"Jesus!" he yelped, his hand snapping back in surprise.

Laughing—*laughing*—Murph climbed up into the shotgun seat.

"It's not funny," he began, but she just kept cackling. He started to scold her again, then he chuckled.

Then he laughed, too.

"You wouldn't be here if it wasn't for me," she pointed out, after her giggles died down.

It felt good, he realized. Laughing with her. Sharing this with her.

He still didn't like putting her in danger, but this might be a good thing in the long run, this little road trip together.

Cooper handed her the map.

"Fair enough," he said, suppressing one last chuckle. "Make yourself useful."

Up ahead, far across the plain, the mountains lay slumped on the horizon—and somewhere among those peaks, they would find their destination. He figured they'd be there by dark.

Murph fell asleep a little before they entered the foothills. He glanced at her in the light of dusk, at the features that so oddly mingled his with her mother's. He wondered, briefly, who she would become, who she would be.

Not a farmer, he was sure of that. Not a farmer's wife. Not even in this "caretaker" world of theirs, where people gradually got used to fewer and fewer choices, until there were none at all.

He shifted his attention again to the dark foothills, his mind turning back to the binary code that had infested his house. Did it really make sense? Was he reading meaning into a random pattern?

How could anyone refuse to believe mankind had gone to the moon?

He didn't blame Murph for taking a poke at those kids.

Cooper took a turn, and then another, winding his way along a narrow road. They were in a mountain pass as night fell complete, and his old friends the stars began looking down through the thinner air of the mountains. Then he felt a yearning that he almost thought he'd forgotten. He felt as if he had somehow left the world he knew, heading for an earlier, younger one. In the dark, with mountains all around and no corn anywhere to be seen, it might have been twenty years ago, or more.

It could have been anytime. Except for the girl, sleeping in the passenger's seat. Time's arrow made visible.

He was still considering the tyranny of entropy when he arrived at the coordinates. He was there—or as near there as he could get with a chain-link fence in his way.

He stared at it for a moment, wondering why this place, why here? He didn't see anything special beyond the barrier, certainly nothing cosmic enough to warrant a message written in gravity. But this was it—the moment when he would learn whether he was inspired or delusional.

The answer lay just yards away. And it was denied to him by the fence.

His daughter was still asleep.

"Murph," he said, gently. "Murph." She opened her eyes and looked groggily around, struggling to sit up.

He nodded at the fence.

"I think this is as far as we get."

Murph glanced at the fence and then closed her eyes again.

"Why?" she asked sleepily. "You didn't bring the bolt cutters?"

He felt a smile broaden his face. That was his girl.

"I like your spirit, young lady," he said.

He exited the cab and got the bolt cutters out of the back, feeling the palm-slicked wood of the handles, cool to the touch. He looked either way, up and down the road, but there was no light, no sound, only the quiet of a mountain night. He reached out with the cutters, laying their steel jaws to the fence...

Blinding light exploded and he threw his hands up to protect his eyes. A voice boomed, harsh, artificial— electronic.

"Step away from the fence."

He dropped the cutters and threw his hands up in the air. He still couldn't see anything but the glare of the spotlights.

"Don't shoot!" he hollered. "My child is in the car! I'm unarmed! My daughter is—"

From the car, Murph heard a sharp snapping sound and instantly sat upright. She saw a flash of actinic blue light as her father jerked, and then dropped like a sack of grain. She felt the car tremble and heard the thud of massive footfalls as she scrambled back in the seat, trying to think—trying *not* to think about what had just happened to her dad...

The door was suddenly yanked open, and blinding light poured in.

"Don't be afraid," a weird, inhuman voice said.

But she was, and she screamed.

NINE

Cooper woke to brightness. Not sunlight. Not the glare of the floodlights—no, this was what he remembered from his youth in government buildings, supermarkets, hospitals.

Institutional lighting.

Everything around him fit with it, too. Each surface was clean, polished, maintained—and uncannily dust-free. And the air smelled funny. Or rather, it *didn't* smell. Not at all. He was so used to the smell of dust and blight that they only became truly apparent by their absence. The air he was breathing now was filtered, scrubbed. Clean.

If he was forced to guess, he imagined he was in some sort of industrial complex.

Yet that was impossible.

He was sitting in a chair, facing a big grey rectangular slab of metal with many dozens of articulated segments—a cuboid of lots of smaller cuboids, like the blocks he'd had as a kid that snapped together to build things.

The machine had a data screen near the top.

Memories began to whirl. He remembered the shock jolting through his body. He remembered...

Murph!

He cast about frantically, looking for his daughter.

"*How did you find this place?*" the slab asked in its electronic voice. The voice from the chain-link fence.

"Where's my daughter?" Cooper demanded. His whole body was prickling with fear now, and anger.

"*You had the coordinates for this facility marked on your map,*" the machine said, ignoring his question. "*Where did you get them?*"

Cooper leaned toward the thing.

"Where's my *daughter!*" he bellowed, but the machine didn't answer. Cooper studied it a little more, collecting himself.

"You might think you're still in the marines," he told it, "but the marines don't exist anymore, pal. I've got grunts like you mowing my grass…"

Suddenly the two outer sections of the machine lengthened and the central slab leaned forward, so now it looked like a fat rectangle standing on thick, blocky crutches. Coming down on him.

"*How did you find us?*" it demanded.

"But you don't look like a lawn mower to me," Cooper plowed on. "You, I'm gonna turn into an overqualified vacuum cleaner—"

"No, you're not," a woman's voice told him.

Cooper turned.

The woman was thirty-something, with short brown hair, wide dark eyes and an expressive mouth. She wore a black sweater and she seemed—like the place—very clean.

"Tars," she said to the machine, "back down, please."

The old military device complied, its "limbs" folding back into the torso to become a cuboid once more.

Cooper considered the woman, looking for some clue as to who she might be, who she represented. Had he stumbled upon some sort of illegal operation? Unfortunately, that would account for a lot of the facts on the ground. The secrecy, the hidden robots, the threat to his person—Murph's disappearance. But how did that fit with the bizarre message on the bedroom floor?

And what were they doing? Manufacturing arms, maybe? Was there a nation someplace, ready to break the international disarmament treaty? He knew things were tough, but surely everyone knew by now that a return to war would only make things worse.

What if it was his own government running this show? That was actually the worst-case scenario, he realized. Maybe the message on Murph's floor hadn't been meant to draw him here, but to warn him away. Maybe it had something to do with the drone.

The woman was studying him, as well, and didn't seem all that impressed by what she saw. That kind of pissed him off.

"You're taking a risk using ex-military for security," he told her. "They're old, their control units are unpredictable."

"Well, that's what the government could spare," she said.

The government. Well, that answered one question. It wasn't the answer he wanted. But at least she was talking.

"Who are you?" Cooper demanded.

"Dr. Brand," she replied.

Cooper paused. The name was familiar.

"I knew a Dr. Brand once," he said tentatively. "But he was a professor—"

"What makes you think I'm not?" she interrupted, frowning at him.

"—and nowhere near as cute," he finished.

An expression falling somewhere between incredulity and disgust crossed her face.

"You think you can *flirt* your way out of this mess?" she said.

What the hell was I thinking? he wondered frantically. Suddenly, his fear for Murph was stronger than ever. He was in *waaaay* over his head, and bluster wasn't going to do him any good.

The problem was, he wasn't sure how to approach any of this. It was too sudden, too disorienting, and he couldn't shake the images of what might have happened or be happening to his daughter. He'd felt something like this before, over the Straights, when the computer had ejected him from his aircraft.

Helpless. Not steering his own ship.

He had to focus his thoughts.

"Dr. Brand," he said quietly, "I have no idea what this 'mess' is. I'm scared for my little girl, and I want her by my side. Then I'll tell you anything you want to know." He paused to let that sink in. "Okay?"

It felt to him like she considered his plea for a long time before turning back to the machine.

"Get the principals and the girl into the conference room," she said, before returning her attention to Cooper. "Your daughter's fine," she said. "Bright kid. Must have a *very* smart mother."

As Brand led him down a corridor, Cooper was acutely aware that the robot was there, too, only a pace or so behind him—well within striking distance. And for all of his talk of turning the thing into a toaster or whatever, he knew that in a straight-up fight he didn't have the slightest chance against it. It could split his skull with a single economical motion.

So there was no point in worrying about it. Instead, he put his mind to sussing out where they were. Or, perhaps more importantly, what this place had been built to accomplish.

Whatever it was, Cooper realized, the amount of time they'd spent walking said that it was *big*—bigger than an arms factory needed to be. Unless they were building nukes, and the ICBMs required to send them out.

That might explain it. Running with the thought, he began to build scenarios. A neutron bomb detonated over, say, the Ukrainian breadbasket, would kill the crops and all of the farmers—and the fields could be used again within a year or two. *More food for team America.*

Could that be the mission? He really didn't want to believe it.

And yet, there were lots of corridors going off in all directions. They had to go *somewhere*. He didn't see any windows, skylights, or doors that showed the outside world, though. So were they underground?

It seemed the likely explanation. Otherwise, *someone* would have stumbled upon this place a long time ago. And an underground facility would be perfect for building big, nasty, unethical things. Hell, this could even be one of the old NORAD installations, replete with the remains of a once-vast nuclear arsenal.

He'd never heard anything about a base being located in this particular mountain range, but what he didn't know about the old Cold War would fill volumes of books.

The more he saw, the less reassured he was. Even if it *was* underground, a place like this would need supplies. To hide something this big would take a certain of amount of… determination. Attention to detail.

He thought again of the military robot clanking along behind him, always within arm's reach.

"It's pretty clear you don't want visitors," he said. "Why not let us back up from your fence, and be on our way?"

"It's not that simple," Brand said.

"Sure it is," he said, trying not to sound panicky. "I don't know anything about you or this place."

"Yes, you do," she countered. Which didn't sound good at all, because that meant even knowing the coordinates was too much.

TEN

After a bit more fretting and walking, they arrived at their destination. It was a typical, old-fashioned conference room, with a series of photos on the walls and a large table in the middle. No window, of course.

She ushered him in.

There were several people present, but the only one who came into focus for him was Murph. Still alive, *thank God*, and apparently in one piece. At least for the moment.

But he couldn't shake the sense that they were deep underground, that no one knew where they were, and that if they went missing, no one would ever know why. Tom would take over the farm, and Donald would help as long as he was able. People would wonder a little what had happened to old Cooper and his daughter.

"Probably just got buried in a dust storm," most would say. People didn't have a lot of time or tolerance for mysteries these days.

An old man was crouched down next to Murph, talking to her. She looked up when he came in.

"Dad!" she shouted, and she bounded across the room into his arms. For a moment he was lost in just having her there, but when he saw the old man stand and smile at him, recognition struck him almost physically.

"Hello, Cooper," the man said.

For a moment he couldn't say anything.

"Professor Brand?" he finally managed.

"Just take a seat, Mr. Cooper," one of the men at the table—youngish, with black hair and a beard—said. Professor Brand remained silent.

Head reeling, Cooper did as he was asked, drawing up a seat. Murph sat beside him. There were five other people sitting at the table. One—an older fellow with glasses and an air of authority—leaned toward them.

"Explain how you found this facility," he demanded.

"Stumbled across it," Cooper lied. "Looking for salvage and I saw the fence—"

The man held up a hand and stopped him. The tight wrinkles that formed his face clinched into disapproving lines.

"You're sitting in the world's best-kept secret," he said. "You don't stumble in. And you certainly don't stumble *out*."

"Cooper, please," Professor Brand said, his voice as even and soothing as it had been decades before. "Cooperate with these people."

The professor was a good guy, at least as Cooper remembered him. Not the sort of man who would end up in anything unsavory. But there were a great many things he once thought of as true.

Still, when he looked at Professor Brand, he *wanted* to trust him.

Maybe the truth is our best bet, Cooper thought. But as he examined the unfriendly faces surrounding him, he realized how crazy the truth was going to sound.

"It's hard to explain," he began, "but we learned these

coordinates from an anomaly…"

"What sort of anomaly?" another man demanded. It was the black-haired fellow who had first told Cooper to sit down. There was an intensity about the question, and as soon as it was asked, everyone else at the table seemed to become a little more alert.

"I don't want to term it 'supernatural,'" Cooper said, "but…"

A couple of them looked away in what appeared to be frustration. Whatever it was they wanted to hear, he wasn't saying it. Then the man with the glasses leaned forward again, his face and tone deadly serious.

"You're going to have to be specific, Mr. Cooper," he said. "Real quick."

Okay, here goes…

"After the last dust storm," Cooper said. "It was a pattern… in dust…"

"It was *gravity*," Murph stated flatly.

And suddenly everyone was gawking at his daughter, as excited as kids on Christmas morning. The black-haired man—the young, bearded one without glasses—looked at Professor Brand, then turned to Cooper.

"Where *was* this gravitational anomaly?" he asked.

Again, Cooper ran his gaze around the room.

"Look," he said, cautiously, "I'm happy you're excited about gravity, but if you want more answers from us I'm gonna need assurances."

"Assurances?" the bespectacled man said.

Cooper covered Murph's ears with his palms. She gave him a look, but he ignored it.

"That we're getting out of here," he whispered fiercely. "And not in the trunk of some car."

Suddenly the younger Dr. Brand began… laughing. Whatever reaction Cooper was expecting, that wasn't it.

Even the man with the glasses smiled.

"Don't you know who we are, Coop?" Professor Brand looked at him, apparently bemused. Cooper began to think everyone but him knew the joke.

"No," Cooper said, feeling like he was going out of his mind. "No, I don't."

Brand—the pretty one—pointed around the table.

"Williams," she said, naming the man with the glasses. Then she continued, "Doyle, Jenkins, Smith. You already know my father, Professor Brand.

"We're NASA."

"NASA?"

"NASA," Professor Brand affirmed. "Same NASA you flew for."

Everyone chuckled, and suddenly Cooper was laughing, too. Relief washed through him like a clear spring of water. Then he glanced at Murph, who looked confused, not getting the gist of it at all.

But then one of the walls began to open, and through the gap, Cooper saw something he had never imagined he would see again. The flared exhaust nozzles of a booster rocket.

"I heard you got shut down for refusing to drop bombs from the stratosphere onto starving people," Cooper said to Professor Brand as they entered the chamber with the spacecraft and passed on through to another part of the complex.

The professor shook his head.

"When they realized killing other people wasn't the long-term solution, they needed us back," he said. "Set us up in the old NORAD facility. In secret."

Well, I was right about the NORAD part, at least.

"Why secret?" Cooper asked.

"Public opinion won't allow spending on space exploration," the professor said. "Not when we're struggling to put food on the table."

That's why so much effort has been put into convincing folks that the space program was a myth, a scam, Cooper realized with sudden clarity. He remembered again the conversation with Murph's teacher, Miss Hanley. What was it she had said? *"Our children need to learn about this planet. Not tales of leaving it."*

As if the Earth existed without the sun, the planets, the stars, the rest of the universe. As if staring harder at the dirt would give them all the answers they needed.

They approached a large door. Professor Brand opened it, and waved him through.

Like everything he had encountered in the last twenty-four hours, what greeted Cooper wasn't what he was expecting. It took him a moment, in fact, to grasp what he was seeing. His first impression was of being outside, but it took only heartbeats for that notion to fade. Instead, he found himself looking at the largest greenhouse complex he had ever seen. Fields the size of plantations, all under glass.

"Blight," the professor said. "Wheat seven years ago, okra this year. Now there's just corn."

Something about that stung a little. He was, after all, a farmer.

"But we're growing more now than ever," he protested.

"Like the potatoes in Ireland, like the wheat in the dust bowl, the corn *will* die," Professor Brand said. "Soon."

Behind them, the young Dr. Brand entered with Murph, who looked around in undisguised awe. Cooper had seen places like this, albeit long ago. Murph had never seen anything of the kind.

She also looked bleary-eyed.

"Murph is a little tired," the younger Brand said. "I'm taking her to my office for a nap."

Cooper nodded, a little relieved. This was probably a conversation his daughter did not need to hear.

"We'll find a way," Cooper objected, once she was out of earshot. "We always have."

"Driven by the unshakable faith that the Earth is ours," Professor Brand added, a bit sarcastically.

"Not *just* ours," Cooper said. "But it is our home."

The professor regarded him coolly.

"Earth's atmosphere is 80 percent nitrogen," he pointed out. "We don't even breathe nitrogen." He pointed to a stalk of corn. The leaves were blotched and striped with grey, which along with the ashen, tumescent blobs of infected kernels were the telltale signs of infection.

"Blight does," the professor continued. "And as it thrives, our air contains less and less oxygen." He gestured toward Murph. "The last people to starve will be the first to suffocate. Your daughter's generation will be the last to survive on Earth."

Cooper stared at him. He wanted to continue to protest, to advocate for hope. New strains of corn could be bred. The answer to the blight might come the day after tomorrow. Human beings were resourceful—it was their hallmark as a race.

But in the pith of him, he knew that everything Professor Brand was saying was true. Unbidden, he experienced an image of Murph, gasping for breath, her eyes, mouth and nostrils caked with dust…

He turned to the professor.

"Tell me this is where you explain how you're going to save the world," he said.

* ✳ *

Their next stop was another room, this one on a scale that dwarfed even the last. But this time he knew instantly what he was seeing, and it brought long-buried feelings rushing back, hard.

It was a multi-stage rocket—a big one—contained in a vastly *larger* cylindrical chamber. In fact, the launch chamber seemed far larger than necessary, by several orders of magnitude. He felt like an ant in a grain silo. High, high above, light shone, this time unmistakably that of the sun, reflected in by a ring of mirrors.

From the look of things, it appeared to be dawn outside.

"We're not meant to save the world," Professor Brand said. "We're meant to *leave* it."

Cooper couldn't take his eyes off of the rocket. He let his gaze travel up, taking in every beautiful inch of her, not in a hurry. When he reached the top he saw two sleek craft mounted there, belly-to-belly, and he knew them.

"Rangers," he murmured. Lineal descendants of the rocket planes like the X-15, and the space shuttles that followed, the winged Rangers could maneuver easily in an atmosphere. Unlike their predecessors, however, they were equally suited for deep space—at least in theory. None of them had ever made it there before the program was cut.

Or so he had believed. So he had been told when he was forced to retire, sent to "do his duty" in the fields, almost two decades ago.

"The last components of our one versatile ship in orbit, the *Endurance*," Professor Brand said. "Our final expedition."

Final, Cooper thought, in a daze. That suggested others. And there had been a fair number of craft in his day. He'd assumed they'd been broken up and recast as farm equipment. But now...

"What happened to the other vehicles?" Cooper asked.

A new, unreadable expression played across the old man's face.

"The Lazarus missions," he said.

"Sounds cheerful," Cooper replied.

"Lazarus came back from the dead—" Dr. Brand began.

"He had to die in the first place," Cooper interjected. "You sent people out there looking for a new home...?" He trailed off, incredulous, but Professor Brand just nodded as if it all made perfect sense.

"There's no planet in our solar system that can support life," Cooper said. "And it'd take them a thousand years to reach the nearest star. That doesn't even qualify as *futile*..." He shook his head. "Where did you send them, Professor?"

"Cooper," Professor Brand said, "I can't tell you any more unless you agree to pilot this craft."

Cooper stared at him, dumbfounded.

"You're the best we ever had," the older man added.

What was he talking about? It had been decades. Everything Cooper had experienced, through most of his adult life, told him this whole thing was impossible. And yet...

To be asked to participate sent an undeniable thrill through him.

Which in turn made him more cautious than ever.

"I barely left the stratosphere," Cooper objected.

"This crew's never left the *simulator*," the professor said. "We can't program this mission from Earth, and we don't know what's out there. We need a pilot. And this is the mission you were trained for."

Cooper thought back to his training. Sure as hell no one had ever mentioned anything like this to him. He'd thought Mars, maybe, or Europa at the outside.

"Without ever knowing," he said. "An hour ago, you didn't even know I was still alive. And you were going anyway."

"We had no choice," Professor Brand said. "But

something brought you here. *They* chose you."

He felt a little chill at that, remembering Murph's ghost, the lines in the dust, the coordinates that showed him the way to this place and these people. In the back of his mind, he'd thought he would find the mysterious messenger here, but by now it was clear that wasn't the case.

Yet from the professor's words, he understood that there *was* a messenger. It wasn't all some figment of his imagination.

"Who's 'they'?" he asked.

But the professor fell silent. Cooper knew the drill. The man had baited the hook, and he was biding his time until the fish was firmly on the line.

Cooper thought about it, about the impossibility—and the possibility—of what the professor was saying.

"How long would I be gone?" he finally asked.

"Hard to know," Brand said. "Years."

"I've got my kids, professor," he said.

The professor nodded, then looked up, solemn and serious.

"Get out there and save them," he said.

Years, Cooper thought. *Years. And yet, the chance to do this*. To live in a dream that had almost faded away; to go out there, push at the boundaries of what was known. To do something that could save his kids, save everyone…

But years?

He met the professor's gaze.

"Who's 'they'?" he repeated.

ELEVEN

Back in the conference room, an image of the solar system appeared on the screen, and a fellow who had been introduced to him as Romilly stood next to it.

He was a young man with a smooth, almost polished scalp, a close-cropped beard, black hair and striking dark features. He couldn't be older than thirty-five. He seemed shy, and spoke in an odd, clipped, almost distracted fashion.

"We started detecting gravitational anomalies almost fifty years ago," Romilly said. "Mostly small distortions in the upper atmosphere—I believe you encountered one yourself."

At first Cooper assumed Romilly meant the pattern in Murph's room, but then the "upper atmosphere" part registered, and his eyes widened as it came back to him.

His instruments going crazy.

Controls ripped from his hands…

"Over the Straights," he blurted. "My crash—something tripped my fly-by wire."

"Exactly," Romilly said. "But the most significant anomaly was *this*…" Saturn suddenly took front and center, with its banded, ochre clouds, expansive rings, and mysterious moons. But when Romilly zoomed in, it wasn't on the planet or any of its satellites, but on a small group of stars.

As the magnification increased, Cooper could see they were rippling, as if seen through a perturbed pool of water.

"A disturbance in space-time, out near Saturn," Romilly said.

Cooper studied the disfigured constellations.

"A wormhole?" Cooper asked, doubtfully. It just didn't seem possible.

"It appeared forty-eight years ago," Romilly confirmed.

A *wormhole*, his brain repeated. A *wormhole!*

There were two essential problems with star travel. The first was that space was big—really big. Things were really far apart. The nearest star to Earth, other than the sun, was so far away that it took light more than four years to make the trip.

A starship traveling at half the speed of light would require more than sixteen years to make the round trip to their nearest stellar neighbor, Proxima Centauri. But that was moot, because no ship he was aware of could go even the tiniest significant fraction of the speed of light.

So a trip to Proxima would take tens of thousands of years for any ship humanity had ever built. Other stars— the ones more likely to have life-bearing planets—were much, much further away.

But a wormhole… That was the northwest passage of star travel—or more aptly, the Panama Canal—the shortcut that meant you didn't have to sail all the way around Cape Horn or the Cape of Good Hope, just to get from Hong Kong to New York.

Except a wormhole was *better* than that. It was a tunnel that just cut through all of that bothersome distance separating one place from another. And you did it in a fraction of the travel time. Relativity predicted wormholes, he remembered, but no one had ever seen one. They remained in the realm of theory.

Or so he'd thought. Yet here he was looking at one.

"Where does it lead?" Cooper asked.

"Another galaxy," Romilly said.

Another galaxy? Cooper tried to bend that through his mind. Those distorted stars didn't belong to Earth's sky, or to the sky of any planet in the Milky Way. That, at least, was what Romilly was claiming. On one level, the very idea seemed preposterous. Yet these people seemed very serious about it indeed.

And there was something else. Something he remembered from his studies, back in the day.

"A wormhole isn't a naturally occurring phenomenon," Cooper said.

It was Dr. Brand who responded.

"Someone placed it there," she agreed, trying to suppress a smile, her dark eyes challenging him to believe her.

"'They,'" he said.

She nodded. "And whoever 'they' are, they appear to be looking out for us," she said. "That wormhole lets us travel to other stars. It came along right as we needed it."

"They've put potentially habitable worlds within our reach," Doyle put in, excitement tangible in his voice. "Twelve, in fact, judging from our initial probes."

"You sent probes into it?" Cooper asked.

"We sent *people* into it," Professor Brand said. "Ten years ago."

"The Lazarus missions," Cooper guessed.

Professor Brand rose and gestured at the walls of the conference room, where twelve portraits hung. Cooper had noticed them before, but hadn't studied them in detail.

They all were of astronauts, garbed in white spacesuits,

sans masks, with the American flag and NASA logo on their shoulders. He had assumed the portraits dated to decades ago, but now he realized he didn't recognize any of their faces. These were astronauts he could not name.

"Twelve possible worlds," the professor said. "Twelve Ranger launches carrying the bravest humans ever to live, led by the remarkable Dr. Mann."

Doyle picked up from there. In contrast with Romilly, Doyle had a sort of focused intensity.

"Each person's landing pod had sufficient life support for two years," he explained, "but they could use hibernation to stretch that, making observations on organics over a decade or more. Their mission was to assess their world, and if it was showing promise, send a signal, bed down for a long nap, and wait to be rescued."

Cooper tried to imagine that. Alone, inconceivably far away from home, gambling everything on finding one habitable world out of twelve.

"And if their world didn't show promise?" Cooper asked.

"Hence the bravery," Doyle replied.

"Because you don't have the resources to visit all twelve," Cooper said.

"No," Doyle confirmed. "Data transmission back through the wormhole is rudimentary—simple binary 'pings' on an annual basis, to give some clue as to which worlds have potential." He paused, then added, "One system shows promise."

"One?" Cooper said. "Kind of a long shot."

Doyle shook his head, and his blue eyes flashed confidence.

"One system with three potential worlds," Dr. Brand said. "No long shot."

Cooper paused a moment to let it sink in. Three worlds, each—or all—offering potential new homes. Hope for his children and grandchildren. But if this ship, this *Endurance* was the only remaining deep-space vessel…

"So if we find a new home," he asked, "what then?"

Professor Brand shot him an approving look.

"*That's* the long shot," he said. "There's plan A, and there's plan B. Did you notice anything strange about the launch chamber?"

The first time Cooper had been in the launch chamber, all he had been able to see was the rocket boosters and the Rangers perched upon it. Sure, he had off-handedly noticed that the chamber was a little bigger than it needed to be. But now, as he really studied it, he realized it was *huge*. Mind-bogglingly so.

It was shaped and proportioned something like a traditional grain silo, but if it was scaled down to the *size* of a grain silo, the Rangers and their boosters would become little more than largish models. The actual circumference of the upright cylinder looked to be as much as a third of a mile.

Hell, it might be more.

Though that was unusual, it wasn't really the strangest part—not by far. The walls of the vast cylinder weren't smooth, the way a normal launch silo would be. Normally, a silo's main function was to shield the rest of the compound from a launch or—in the worst-case scenario—an explosion. So there would be no protuberances.

High above where he stood, several odd structures had been built onto the interior surface—were still being constructed, in fact. He couldn't imagine what they were, though, or what their uses might be. Some almost looked like buildings, but jutting out at weird angles that would make them unusable.

Suddenly his perspective shifted, and dizzyingly. What if the structures actually *were* buildings? Houses, schools, other facilities. At the very thought, their purposes became clear. And yet, they were built along the curve, horizontal to the ground, useless...

On Earth, he thought. *They'd be useless here on Earth. With a planetary gravity.* But in space, with the vast cylinder spinning along its axis, "down" would be relative. The entire inner surface of the cylinder would become the ground on which folks would walk.

"This whole facility," he began, still not quite believing what he was saying, "it's a vehicle? A space station?"

"Both," Professor Brand said. "We've been working on it—and others like it—for twenty-five years. Plan A."

Cooper ran his gaze around the inside-out world that was still a work in progress. He'd seen designs for things like this, but they were meant to be built in space, not beneath the surface of a planet.

"How does it get off the Earth?" he asked. It seemed undoable. Even if there were thrusters powerful enough to push it into orbit, the entire structure would break up under the acceleration. No object so large could handle the force necessary to escape Earth's pull.

"Those first gravitational anomalies changed everything," Professor Brand explained. "Suddenly we knew that harnessing gravity was real. So I started working on the theory—and we started building this station."

Cooper heard something in the professor's tone.

"But you haven't solved it yet," he guessed, and the older man nodded grimly.

"That's why there's a plan B," Dr. Brand said, her dark eyes studying him. Weighing him up, maybe? Trying to decide if he was worthy?

She motioned, and led Cooper to a nearby lab full of

devices built for purposes he couldn't even guess. They came to a stop in front of a vault made of glass and steel. It housed a series of movable shelves fronted by circular white seals. Dr. Brand grasped a handle on one and turned. The seal opened and she pulled out a cylindrical steel unit housing a multitude of glass vials.

Condensation sighed out from the now empty cavity, like a breath on a cold day.

"The problem is gravity," she said. "How to get a viable amount of human life off this planet. This is one way. Plan B—a population bomb. Almost five thousand fertilized eggs, preserved in containers weighing in at under nine hundred kilos."

Five thousand children, he thought. *Five thousand, in this little vault, waiting to be brought into the world.*

"How could you raise them?" Cooper asked.

"With equipment on board, we incubate the first ten," Brand replied, as if she was talking about planting corn. "After that, with surrogacy, the growth becomes exponential. Within thirty years, we might have a colony of hundreds. The real difficulty of colonization is genetic diversity." She pointed to the glass vials enclosed by the device. "This takes care of that."

Cooper looked at the thing, an uncomfortable feeling growing in the back of his mind. Genetic diversity, sure— five thousand fertilized eggs could be selected to represent the entire range of human variation. Efficient, maybe, but it was clinical, cold. And it presented one huge problem.

"So we just give up on people here?" he asked.

"That's why plan A's a lot more fun," Dr. Brand said.

Cooper thought about the huge Earthbound station. How much had it cost? What a massive gamble—every dime spent here was a dime *not* being spent trying to beat the blight, to feed the people of the planet. Was the professor really that sure he could pull this out of his hat? He seemed to have convinced all of the right people that he could.

Maybe the professor is right, he mused. *He knows a helluva lot more than I do about the big picture.* Maybe whoever was studying the blight had decided it couldn't be fought—that, as Professor Brand said, it was just a matter of time. Maybe they were spending resources on this project because, no matter how far-fetched the whole thing seemed, it was the only hope humanity had.

A lot of really smart people had to have bought into the idea.

Of course, even smart people can be wrong.

Still, it was all better than what he had feared at first. They hadn't turned back to weapons, thank God, and war. He hadn't stumbled onto a plan to take what little was left and hoard it away. They weren't trying to squeeze the last remaining drops of life from the dirt.

No, instead of looking down, they were looking up.

They had turned back to the stars.

Later, Professor Brand showed him the equations. Cooper had had plenty of math back in the day, but it had been more applied than theoretical, so this was all way beyond him. The equations covered more than a dozen blackboards in the professor's office, complete with diagrams, and while he could pick out parts of it, the rest might as well have been written in cuneiform, as far as he was concerned.

"Where have you got to?" Cooper asked.

"Almost there," Professor Brand assured him.

"Almost? You're asking me to hang everything on 'almost?'"

The professor stepped a little closer.

"I'm asking you to trust me," he said. Professor Brand's eyes were burning with what seemed like a limitless passion, and Cooper realized that the old man had thrown all of himself into this. He believed—*really* believed—that it could be done. Cooper had seen glimpses of this fervor before, back in the day, but he had never understood what lay behind it.

Now he did. The survival of the human race.

"All those years of training," he said. "You never told me."

"We can't always be open about *everything*, Coop, even if we want to be." The professor paused, and then he said, "What can you tell your children about this mission?"

That was a tender point, one he had already been considering. What *would* he tell Tom and Murph? That the world was ending? That he was going off into space to try and save it? And if he had known all those years ago he was training for such a mission, how would he have reacted?

There was no way to know. So much time had passed, so much had occurred, he barely knew the young man he had once been.

"Find us a new home," the professor said. "When you return, I'll have solved the problem of gravity. You have my word."

TWELVE

The truck had barely rolled to a stop before Murph swung the door open and dashed for the house. On the porch, Donald watched her whiz past, then shot his son-in-law a questioning look.

Cooper simply shook his head and followed Murph inside and up the stairs. He heard a dragging sound coming from her room.

When he tried to open her door, it only cracked a little—from what he could tell, she had stacked a desk and a chair against it.

"Murph?" he attempted.

"Go!" she shouted. "If you're leaving, just go!"

Donald listened in his usual way, without many interruptions or much expression, just taking it in as it came. It was a little cool on the porch, but Cooper preferred to be out beneath the night sky, rather than in the house.

After a time, he'd given Donald the full story of what had happened to him and Murph. He sat back to see how the old man would react.

"This world was never enough for you, was it, Coop?" Donald said.

Cooper didn't answer right away. He knew it was an indictment, that there was an accusation there. Donald took things as they came. He might grouse a little here and there, but he was adaptable. And he was good at finding the virtue in whatever situation presented itself. He was a man who counted his blessings more often than he railed against injustice.

Nothing wrong with that, Cooper mused. The world needed people like Donald, and always had. But it needed more than one kind of person. It needed the men who sailed dangerous seas, to discover unknown lands. Those men had not been—for the most part—of the "count-your-blessings" sort.

"I'm not gonna lie to you, Donald," Cooper said. "Heading out there is what I feel born to do, and it excites me. That doesn't make it wrong."

Donald thought about that for a moment.

"It might," the old man countered. "Don't trust the right thing, done for the wrong reason. The 'why' of a thing—that's the foundation."

"Well, the foundation's solid," Cooper said, a bit sadly. He swept his hand out toward the fields, the distant mountains—the world.

"We farmers sit here every year when the rains fail and say 'next year.'" He paused, and looked at his father-in-law. "Next year ain't gonna save us. Nor the one after. This world's a treasure, Donald. But she's been telling us to leave for a while now. Mankind was born on Earth. It was never meant to die here."

He stopped, feeling somehow a little hollow, even though he believed everything he said. He was right, and Donald would get to that.

So would the kids.

Donald brushed some dust off of the porch rail. He pursed his lips, and now he did seem emotional—uncharacteristically so.

"Tom'll be okay," he said, as if reading Cooper's mind. "But you have to make it right with Murph…"

"I will," Cooper said, even though he knew it was easier said than done.

"*Without* making any promises you don't know you can keep," Donald finished, looking him directly in the eye.

Cooper looked away, nodding.

Feeling the burden.

Cooper figured he'd let Murph cool down overnight, that she'd be easier to approach after some sleep. But the next morning, the door was still barricaded. He pressed it open gingerly, until he could reach the chair and pull it down from where it was stacked on the desk. Then he pushed it wider and stepped in.

Murph was in her bed, back turned to him.

"You have to talk to me," he said.

She didn't respond, and he wondered if she might still be asleep.

"I have to fix this before I go," he said.

He leaned over her to see her face, and he felt a sort of shock go through him. Her cheeks were still blazing and tear-stained, and he wondered if she'd slept at all.

"Then I'll keep it broken," she said stubbornly. "So you have to stay."

So that's how it's gonna be.

Cooper sat on the bed. He had taken Donald's advice to heart, and had been practicing what to say, staying up half the night. He hadn't expected Murph to still be this upset, however. In his mind's-eye rehearsal, he'd been having this conversation with a calmer, quieter daughter.

He still had to give it a go, though, and he thought he knew how to begin.

"After you kids came along," he told her, "your mother said something I didn't really understand. She said, 'I look at the babies and see myself as they'll remember me.'"

He studied Murph to see if it was sinking in.

At least she appeared to be listening. So he continued.

"She said, 'It's as if we don't exist anymore, like we're ghosts, like we're just there to be memories for our kids.'"

He paused again before going on. The expression on Murph's face was a little puzzled—and he didn't blame her. It had taken him a while to get it himself.

"Now I realize," he said, "once we're parents, we're just the ghosts of our children's futures."

"You said ghosts don't exist," Murph replied defiantly.

"That's right," Cooper said. "I can't be your ghost right now—I need to exist. Because they chose me. They chose me, Murph. You saw it."

Murph sat up and pointed at the shelves, at the gaps between the books.

"I figured out the message," she said. She opened her notebook. "It *was* Morse code."

"Murph…" Cooper said, gently.

She ignored him.

"One word," she continued. "You know what it is?"

He shook his head. She held out her notebook so he could see it.

STAY

"It says 'stay,' Dad." She peered at him, waiting for his response.

"Oh, Murph," he said, his voice sad.

"You don't believe me?" she said, her eyes flashing defiantly. "Look at the books. Look at—"

He reached out and took her in his arms, stopping her from saying anymore. She felt so little, and she was trembling.

"It's okay," he told her. "It's okay."

She pressed her face into his shoulder, sobbing.

"Murph," he said, "a father looks in his child's eyes and thinks, 'Maybe it's them. Maybe my child will save the world.' And everyone, once a child, wants to look into their own dad's eyes and know he saw they saved some little corner of the world. But usually, by then, the father is gone."

"Like you will be," she said, and she sniffed. Cooper gazed at his daughter, at the fear and pain written on her face.

"No," he said "I'm coming back." Even as he said it, he understood he'd done just what Donald had told him not to. But he had to say something. To get her through it. To get both of them through it.

To give her hope.

Yet he dreaded her next question.

"When?" she asked.

Murph took little for granted. He knew that, so he was prepared. He reached into his pocket and pulled out two wristwatches.

"One for you," he said, and then pointed to the watch on his wrist. "One for me."

She took the watch, turning it in her hand, examining it curiously.

"When I'm in hypersleep," he explained, "or travel near the speed of light, or near a black hole, time will change for me. It'll run more slowly."

Murph frowned slightly.

"When I get back we can compare," he said, then he waited.

He could almost see her brain working through it.

"Time will run differently for us?" she said. There was a hint of wonderment in her tone, and he felt a little flush of relief. If she could see this as an adventure, *her* adventure as well as his, and understand his promise…

"Yup," he told her. "By the time I get back we might be the same age. You and me. Imagine that."

He watched as her face changed, and he knew he'd made a mistake, said perhaps *exactly* the wrong thing.

"Wait, Murph—"

"You have no idea when you're coming back," she said angrily.

He gave her a pleading look. He needed something to say, but this was off his script.

"No idea at *all*!" she shouted, and she slung the watch across the room before turning her back on him again.

So quickly, what little momentum he'd had—or maybe just imagined he had—was gone. His plan, such as it was, was suddenly was in tatters, and there wasn't any time to start over, even if he knew how.

"Don't make me leave like this," Cooper pleaded.

But her back stayed to him.

"Please," he said. "I have to go now." He reached to put his hand on her shoulder, but she angrily shook it off.

"I love you, Murph," he said, finally. "Forever. And I'm coming back."

Slowly he stood up. Everything about him felt heavy. He knew if he stayed another minute, another hour, another day, it would be the same. Either he was going, or he wasn't. Murph would be okay, and in time she would understand.

As he reached the threshold, he heard a *thunk* behind him. He turned, but Murph was still facing away from him. A newly fallen book lay on the floor. He looked at it for a moment, wondering.

Then, reluctantly, he stepped out of Murph's room.

Donald and Tom met him at the car.

"How'd it go?" Donald asked.

"Fine," Cooper lied. "It was fine."

He turned to Tom and wrapped him up in a tight hug.

"I love you, Tom," he said.

"Travel safe, Dad," his son replied.

"Look after the place, you hear?" he said, feeling a hitch in his voice

"Can I use your truck while you're gone?" Tom asked.

Cooper managed a smile. That was Tom. Practical. Pragmatic. And eager to get his hands on the wheel.

"I'll make sure they bring it back for you," he promised. Then, not wanting to linger, he got in the truck and started the engine.

"Mind my kids for me, Donald," he said.

The old man nodded as he pulled out.

Back in the house, Murph heard the car start. Her anger broke in an instant, dissolving into anguish.

She'd thought he would come back, that he was bluffing. She jumped off the bed, grabbed the watch and ran for the stairs. She had to tell him, had to really say goodbye, to hug him one last time.

* * *

Cooper watched the house dwindle in the rearview mirror. Even now, so much of him wanted to turn back, to be with his children. If only Murph…

A thought occurred to him, and he reached back into the wheel well and pulled up the blanket from where she had hidden last time, but now it was empty. He'd known it would be, yet part of him had needed to *know*.

So he fixed his mind on the Rangers, perched atop their boosters, waiting for him.

And then on the countdown.

Ten, nine…

Murph nearly tripped on the stairs, but then she flew across the kitchen and burst through the door, out onto the porch.

"Dad? *Dad!*" she yelled desperately.

Eight, seven…

All she could see was a dust trail, leading away toward the mountains, as it had before. *But this time she wasn't hiding under the blanket. She wasn't in the truck.*

Six, five…

Great sobs started tearing from her chest as Grandpa took her in his arms, and the trail of dust grew more distant. She gripped the watch in her hand as she cried, willing him to keep his promise, to come back.

Cooper looked once more in the rearview mirror, but all he could see was dust. He felt tears rolling down his cheeks.

Four, three, two…

One.

PART TWO

THIRTEEN

"Ignition!" the flight controller said.

For an instant, Cooper thought that nothing was going to happen, that from the start it had all been some sort of weird hoax or delusion. But then he felt the vibration, the shudder that ran through the whole metal skin of the ship—awful and slow at first, like a titan stirring, but then gathering speed at a dreadful pace.

Then the light was changing, growing brighter, the sky getting closer as a huge invisible hand pressed down on him, harder and harder.

Gagarin, he thought, *Shepard, Grissom, Titov, Glenn, Carpenter, Nikclayev...*

The bright day was already fading as the horizon appeared in his vision. There was a sudden, gut-wrenching lurch, as the hand pressing him down came off for an instant, and his body pulled forward.

Then the G-force slammed him back into his crash couch.

"Stage one, separation," he heard control say. He tried to imagine the huge booster dropping away, but it was hard to think of anything but the force pinning him down, the

barely controlled bomb that lay behind him, hurling him toward the stars.

White, Chaffee, Komarov...

The horizon began to curve in earnest. The ship was no longer shuddering, although it was still humming with acceleration. He couldn't move. He felt as if he weighed a thousand pounds, as if the next time he exhaled he would not be able to inhale again, and he would suffocate in his crash couch.

Then he felt suddenly as if he was falling—almost like he had been hurled from a plane—and then he weighed nothing at all.

"*Stage two, separation,*" control said.

Armstrong, Collins, Aldrin...

Skip ahead, he thought.

Cooper.

Because finally, incredibly—he was in space.

As soon as he could move again, he glanced around the cramped cabin at his companions to see how they were handling things. Dr. Brand, Doyle, and Romilly looked like he probably did—a little dazed.

"All here, Mr. Cooper," the fifth member of the crew assured him. Tars, the robot who had zapped him at the fence. "Plenty of slaves for my robot colony."

Cooper wondered if his ears—or worse, his brain—had been affected by lift-off. His confusion must have been written across his face, because Doyle stepped in.

"They gave him a humor setting," he explained. "So he'd fit in with his unit better. He thinks it relaxes us."

"A massive sarcastic robot," Cooper remarked. "What a good idea."

"I have a cue light I can turn on when I'm joking, if you like," Tars offered.

"Probably help," Cooper said.

"You can use it to find your way back to the ship after I blow you out of the airlock," Tars said.

Tars "looked" at him, and Cooper looked back. He didn't see anything that appeared to be a cue light.

The hairs on the back of his neck were beginning to prick up when an LED suddenly flashed on.

Frowning, Cooper shook his head.

"What's your humor setting, Tars?" he asked.

"One hundred percent," the machine replied.

Wonderful. How many months was it going to be?

"Take it down to seventy-five, please," he said, then he turned away, glanced around to assure himself that everyone was still strapped in, and started checking the instruments.

The conjoined Rangers settled into a low orbit, and for a time there was nothing to do but wait.

Nothing wrong with that, he mused. The Ranger had a wide field of vision, giving them all a panoramic view of Earth as it turned below them. Even though he was still strapped into his crash couch, Cooper found himself rubbernecking like a tourist, watching the continents, seas, and clouds—thinking that it all seemed somehow a little unreal. The lift-off, the terrible acceleration, appeared as if long ago and now, as they spent their time in free-fall, everything felt a dream.

The planet—*his* planet—was as beautiful as it was fragile, and it was the only home humanity had ever known. Viewing it from out here, he found it hard to believe that she didn't want them anymore.

He noticed that Dr. Brand was also watching the world turn below them, her expression distant.

"We'll be back," he told her.

She didn't show any sign that she'd heard him, didn't

turn away from the view, but continued to stare.

"It's hard," he went on. "Leaving everything. My kids, your father…"

"We're going to be spending a lot of time together," Brand said, turning her gaze toward him.

Cooper nodded. "We should learn to talk," he said.

"And when not to," she replied, looking away again. "Just trying to be honest," she added.

"Maybe you don't need to be *that* honest," he said, wincing internally. He looked over at Tars. "Tars, what's your honesty parameter?"

Tars didn't need a crash couch. He fit into a niche in the center of the control panel, between the manual units.

As Cooper spoke, he unlatched himself and moved toward the rear airlock.

"Ninety percent," he responded.

"Ninety?" Cooper said. "What kind of robot are you?"

"Absolute honesty isn't always the most diplomatic — or safe — form of communication with emotional beings," Tars informed him.

True that, Cooper thought wryly. He turned back to Brand, and shrugged.

"Ninety percent honesty it is, then," he said.

At first he thought he had bombed again, but then her lips traced a smile on her face. Almost imperceptible, but he was sure it was there.

Progress.

"*Sixty seconds out…*" The radio crackled.

Cooper decided he'd better quit while he was ahead. Besides, he was about to earn his pay. The first installment, anyway.

So he looked away from the Earth and Brand, and focused his attention on the *Endurance*, as they approached her. His first impression was of a wedding ring, glittering in the twin lights of the Earth and the sun.

The Rangers were sleek, winged, aerodynamic craft built for landing and taking off from planets that possessed atmospheres. Not so the *Endurance*—there was nothing aerodynamic about her, and any landing she made on any planet with an atmosphere would be pretty much the same sort of landing as a meteor would make: fast, fiery, and catastrophic.

Yet floating in space—where she had been built—the vessel was a thing of beauty.

She was, indeed, a ring—but only in the most basic sense, and as they drew nearer his original impression faded. He could distinguish that she was formed from a number of boxy, trapezoidal, prism-shaped modules jointed together by curved connectors. The "ring" wasn't empty either. Access tubes led from the inner surface of the circular body to a central axis where the docking locks lay. Two ships—the landers—were already there. All she needed were the two Rangers. Feeling oddly calm, Cooper maneuvered his Ranger in, matching his velocity to that of the starship.

He'd run through the docking sequence plenty in simulations, but in the back of his mind he'd worried that the real thing would throw him some sort of curve. But he got her lined up with ease, which felt good.

"It's all you, Doyle," he said.

Doyle drifted toward the hatch and began the final sequence, which was sort of the tricky part. If he messed this up they would at best lose precious oxygen and at worst—well, he wasn't sure, but it could be bad. He watched as Doyle lined up a circular array of small grapples and engaged them to bring the two ships together in an airtight seal. Each mechanical claw latched perfectly, as if Doyle had been doing this his whole life.

With that, the *Endurance* was complete.

* ✳ *

Once Amelia Brand's primate brain stopped screaming that she was falling and needed to grab on to something, zero gravity turned out to be great fun. The slightest push sent her flying around effortlessly in a way she had never imagined—not even in her dreams.

It was almost too bad it had to end.

As they boarded the *Endurance*, it became clear that it wasn't as roomy as it looked from the outside. Part of this was because two-thirds of each of the modules was taken up by storage. The floors, the walls—almost every surface was composed of hatches of various sizes. On a deep-space vessel, there could be no wasted space—not even one the size of a matchbox.

Flipping switches and adjusting settings, Amelia, Doyle, and Romilly began powering up what would be their home for—well, who knew how long? She watched Tars activate Case, an articulated machine like himself, who made up the final member of their crew.

Doyle moved "up" to the cockpit and turned on the command console. Technically, there was no up or down at this point, but soon it would no longer be a technicality, as evinced by the ladder that led from the lower deck up to the command deck.

She watched as Doyle finished linking the on-board systems to the Ranger.

"Cooper, you should have control," Doyle said.

"Talking fine," Cooper replied. "Ready to spin?"

Doyle and Romilly strapped in. Amelia followed their lead and took a chair.

"All set," she replied.

She felt nothing at first, but then the ship began to shake as Cooper fired the Ranger's thrusters, angled perfectly to set the great wheel turning. As the spin picked up, weight began to return to Amelia's body, pulling her feet toward the outer rim of the starship. It wasn't gravity, exactly, but the manifestation of inertia often referred to as centrifugal force. Without it—without some semblance of weight—bad things happened to the human body over time, like bone loss and heart disease.

We're going to need our bones and our hearts when we reach our destination, she thought.

Unfortunately, spin wasn't a perfect substitute for gravity, because the inner ear wasn't entirely fooled by it. It knew they were whirling around due to a little thing called the Coriolis effect

On Earth the Coriolis effect was a big deal. It drove the climate, creating huge cells of air moving in circles—clockwise in the northern hemisphere, counter-clockwise in the southern. But the Earth was so huge, the human body didn't notice the spin on a personal level. Yet on a whirling carnival ride it was easy to feel, often with upsetting results.

The *Endurance* lay somewhere in between those extremes, though leaning toward the carnival ride. Amelia felt it herself, especially when she moved toward the axis, but it didn't really bother her.

Romilly, on the other hand, already was looking a little green.

"You okay, there?" she asked him.

"Yup." He practically gurgled as he replied. "Just need a little time—"

"There should be a Dramamine in the hab pod," she told him. He nodded gratefully, and moved gingerly in that direction.

FOURTEEN

"*I miss you already, Amelia,*" Professor Brand told his daughter, via the video link. "*Be safe. Give my regards to Dr. Mann.*"

"I will, Dad," Amelia said.

"*Things look good for your trajectory,*" the professor continued. "*We're calculating two years to Saturn.*"

"That's a lot of Dramamine…" Romilly said. He didn't seem to be getting along with the artificial gravity, yet Cooper hadn't felt even a twinge of unpleasantness.

Two years, though, he thought. Murph would be twelve, and Tom seventeen. And then another two years back to Earth, so really fourteen and nineteen. Minimum. That was what he was going to miss, *if* their mission in the wormhole took zero time.

Which it would not.

Still, maybe it wouldn't take all *that* long. In theory the trip through the wormhole would take a fraction of the time, relatively speaking. Maybe the closest planet would be the one to pan out. He might yet be home while Murph was still in her teens.

"Keep an eye on my family, sir," Cooper told Professor

Brand. "'Specially Murph. She's a smart one."

"We'll be waiting when you get back," the scientist promised. *"A little older, a little wiser, but happy to see you."*

Cooper prepped the engines as Doyle ran a last series of diagnostics from the cockpit cabin of the *Endurance*. It was a little roomier than the one in the Ranger, set above the central cabin and reached by the rungs of a short ladder.

Brand and Romilly strapped in, and Tars and Case likewise secured themselves with metallic *clanks*.

Cooper gazed down at the Earth once more, Professor Brand's last words still fresh in his mind.

"Do not go gentle into that good night…"

He checked with Doyle, who nodded an okay. Then, without any ceremony, he fired the thrusters, and the *Endurance* began its journey out of Earth's orbit, and toward the stars.

"Rage, rage against the dying of the light. Godspeed, Endurance."

"So alone," Cooper said, staring at the diminishing sphere of the Earth. They had all changed into their blue sleep outfits, and had begun setting up the cryo-beds—which looked way too much like fancy coffins for his taste. Brand came to stand next to him.

"We've got each other," she told him. "Dr. Mann had it worse."

"I meant them," he said, pointing at Earth. "Look at that perfect planet. We're not gonna find another one like her."

"No," Brand agreed. "This isn't like looking for a new condo—the human race is going to be adrift, desperate for a rock to cling to while they catch their breaths. We have to find that rock. Our three prospects are at the edge of what might sustain human life."

She held up her tablet and tapped a blurry image of a dark blue planet. The color made it feel promising almost immediately. Blue was what Earth looked like from way out. Blue could mean water. Of course, Neptune was also blue, and it had an atmosphere of hydrogen, helium, and trace methane—completely inimical to life as they knew it.

"Laura Miller's first," Brand said. "She started our biology program."

The image switched to an even smaller image, faintly red. It reminded him of early photographs of Mars.

"And Wolf Edmunds is here," she said. And the way she said it, the way his name came off her tongue—Cooper had never heard anything like that in her voice before. As if that red dot was the center of the universe. Suddenly he was curious.

"Who's Edmunds?" he asked.

"Wolf's a particle physicist," she said, and this time he knew he heard it. And the way she smiled...

Interesting...

"None of them had family?" he asked, pressing from the side rather than the back. He didn't have Brand entirely figured yet, but he'd seen enough to guess that head-on wasn't the right way to come at her.

"No attachments," she replied. "My father insisted. They knew the odds against ever seeing another human being. I'm hoping we surprise at least three of them."

"Tell me about Dr. Mann," he said.

A new world came up on screen, white and grainy.

"Remarkable," she said. "The best of us. My father's protégé. He inspired eleven people to follow him on the loneliest journey in human history." A different sort of passion flared in her eyes, and he saw some of her father there. "Scientists, explorers," she said. "That's what I love. Out there we face great odds. Death. But not evil."

"Nature can't be evil?" Cooper said.

"Formidable," Brand said. "Frightening—not evil. Is a tiger evil because it rips a gazelle to pieces?"

Cooper reflected on that. If you were the gazelle, he mused, it was a moot point what was going on in the tiger's heart and soul—whether it was evil, or just staying alive. Plenty of human beings had justified immensely evil acts in the name of survival and the "natural order of things."

"Just what we bring with us then," he said. He didn't want to get into a real argument, but stubbornly found himself unwilling to let the point slide past completely.

Apparently she noticed.

"This crew represents the best aspects of humanity," Brand said, a little testily, but he let it go. Why start the trip with a pointless philosophical argument? They had to live with one another for a long time.

In fact, he realized, what they had—along with Romilly and Doyle—was a lot like a marriage. They had to make it work, and they didn't have the recourse of separation or divorce if things started to get unpleasant. Friction had to be kept at a minimum.

"Even me?" Cooper asked, trying to lighten things back up.

Brand smiled.

"Hey, we agreed," she said. "Ninety percent." With that she went to her own cryo-bed. Cooper returned his gaze to the infinite space outside of the ship.

"Don't stay up too late," Brand instructed. "We can't spare the resources."

"Hey," Cooper objected with mock chagrin. "I've been waiting a long time to be up here."

"You are *literally* wasting your breath," she said. She got into the bed and lay down. The lid slid shut over her, encasing her in a plastic sheath. Liquid began filling in around the plastic, where it would freeze into a shield that would help protect her from the two years' worth of radiation that would sleet through the hull as she slept.

Sweet dreams, he wished her, and wondered if one did in fact dream in cryo-sleep.

Cooper turned away and went to join Tars.

"Show me the trajectory again," he told the machine. A diagram appeared on the screen.

"Eight months to Mars," Tars said, "just like the last time we talked about it. Then counter-orbital slingshot around—"

Cooper saw Brand's bed darken, then begin withdrawing into the deck.

"Tars," he interrupted, speaking in a whisper. After all, he'd seen the trajectory so often he could draw it blindfolded. He didn't need a bedtime review. But there was something about the… *social* situation on board, and a bit of pertinent information he needed to figure out.

Purely for sociological reasons.

"Tars," he began, "was Dr. Brand—"

"Why are you whispering?" Tars asked. "You can't wake them."

He had been whispering, hadn't he? Why? He knew Tars was right.

Was he embarrassed?

Nah, he decided. *Just being considerate. And this might be important.*

Later.

"Were Dr. Brand and Edmunds… close?" he asked carefully.

"I wouldn't know," Tars replied.

"Is that ninety percent, or ten percent 'wouldn't know?'" Cooper pursued.

"I also have a discretion setting," the robot informed him.

"So I gather," Cooper replied. He stood up. "But not a poker face."

With that he dragged himself reluctantly to the comm station. Everyone else had recorded their goodbyes, but he still didn't know what he was going to say, how he was going to say it. And probably, he had to admit, that was because there was no right thing to say.

Yet he had to say *something*. So after a few moments of hemming and hawing, he tapped the control.

"Hey, guys," he finally began. "I'm about to settle down for a long nap, so I figured I'd send you an update." He looked again at the dwindling jewel of the planet, apparently spinning due to the *Endurance*'s rotation.

"The Earth looks amazing from here. You can't see any of the dust. I hope you guys are doing great. This should get to you okay. Professor Brand said he'd make sure of it." He paused, aching to say more, something that could wipe away his farewell to Murph, and make everything okay.

But he couldn't come up with anything.

"Guess I'll say goodnight," he finished instead.

FIFTEEN

Donald sat on the porch looking out over the cornfields. Dust and heat made the horizon shimmer—which wasn't unusual—but between there and him, something else was coming. In time he saw it was a pair of vehicles.

One of them was Cooper's truck. He hoped…

Then he sighed as the door burst open, and Murph came running out. Of course she had seen them coming. The way she stayed at that window…

"Is it him?" she asked softly.

"I don't think so, Murph," he replied. He could have answered unconditionally, but chose not to. Coop had left her in tears. That had been the hard part for him, leaving his daughter while she was so upset. Yet Donald had known when his son-in-law had left that if he didn't turn around in the first five minutes, he was *never* coming back. But he hadn't, and he wasn't. That Murph still hoped showed that she didn't understand her father as well as Donald did.

He stood up to meet the truck as it pulled up to the house. A man with a decade or so more years than Donald stepped out. He had a look about him, and Donald guessed it was probably the Professor Brand fellow Coop had mentioned.

"You must be Donald," the man said. Then he looked at the girl. "Hello, Murph."

"Why're you in my dad's truck?" she demanded.

"He wanted me to bring it for your brother," the man explained.

Murph didn't reply, and after an awkward silence, the man reached for a briefcase.

"He sent you a message—"

But Murph wasn't having any of that, Donald knew. She spun on her heel and bolted back into the house.

The man hesitated for a moment, then pulled out a disk. He held it out toward Donald, who took it.

"Pretty upset with him for leaving," Donald explained. It was an understatement, but there was no point in being particular, not with these people, this guy.

"If you record messages," the man said, "I'll transmit them to Cooper."

Donald nodded, looking up at the house, thinking that Murph would never do it. He'd bet the farm on it.

"Murph's a bright spark," the man said, following his gaze. "Maybe I could fan the flame."

Donald looked at him, gauged the man's expression, and saw that he was serious. He had something in mind. Then he thought about Murph, still in school, becoming angrier and more belligerent—until she got expelled.

And then what?

"She's already making fools out of her teachers," Donald said. "She should come make a fool out of you."

The man grinned. Donald liked that.

He looked up into the sky.

"Where are they?" he asked.

"Heading toward Mars," the man replied. "The next time we hear from Cooper, they'll be coming up on Saturn."

Donald nodded.

Godspeed, Coop, he thought. *Hope you find what you're looking for. I hope it's worth it. Worth what you left.*

Murph might see Cooper again. Donald was pretty sure he never would

He sighed. He'd already done the father thing, hadn't he? Put in his time?

He was tired.

Count your blessings, old man, he thought to himself. *Some men never even live to see their grandchildren.* There was so little left that had any value to him. Only Murph and Tom, really. What did he have to complain about?

He would rest when he was dead.

SIXTEEN

Mars had been an object of fascination from the earliest days of modern astronomy, in part because it seemed so Earthlike.

Whole civilizations had risen on the red planet—in the imaginations of Lowell, Wells, Weinbaum, Burroughs, and so many other famous authors. Those civilizations had all fallen when the first robotic landers reported the dull truth. If Mars had ever been a place habitable by human beings—or anything like them—it had been a very long time ago. And if there was life there now, it was hiding itself very, very well.

Which is why they had left it behind. Mars wasn't going to be humanity's new home, any more than the Moon was.

Saturn had held the attention and wonder of the world for centuries, as well, but while Mars had done so because it was so Earthlike, Saturn caught the eye because it was so incredibly weird. In movies, in fiction, if you wanted to make clear a planet was really alien, you put rings around it. It was huge, as well, with an atmosphere of mostly hydrogen and helium and clouds of ammonia crystals. No home for humanity there, either, but beauty in plenty, with those bands of ice glittering in the cold light of a distant sun.

Cooper checked his instruments. Dropping into orbit, the *Endurance* became newest of more than one hundred and fifty moons that circled the gas giant—and that wasn't counting the trillions of ice gems that made up the rings.

Or the object of their mission.

He checked the controls again and then went to the comm booth.

Two years.

He wanted to see his kids.

"...but they said I can start advanced agriculture a year early," Tom said, as Cooper sat in the comm booth. He was listening, a blanket wrapped around his shoulders.

It was weird watching him change. Several recordings had been sent, the first just after Cooper went into cryosleep, and the most recent just a few days ago. They were so far away from Earth now that it took around eighty-four minutes for light—or a radio wave—to make the trip, making real-time conversations impossible, since that would mean a lag of nearly three hours between, "Hi, how are you?" and, "I'm good, how about you?"

In space, distance was time, and time was distance.

Tom mostly talked about the farm. He'd had a little trouble with Boots taking him seriously, but Donald had helped him iron that out. He'd met a girl, but that only lasted a few months. Cooper wasn't surprised—he remembered the girl, an only child and a bit of a spoiled princess. Not that people couldn't change, but sometimes there was a whole lot of inertia to overcome if that was to happen.

Tom had managed to repurpose the drone, which was

good, because soon after Cooper left, the farm had lost a third of its solar panels in a black blizzard that had lasted almost thirty hours straight. The good news—according to his son—was that the government considered the storm to be a turning point. From here on out, they claimed, the environment would get better.

He wasn't sure he believed it, but hope was hope.

By the last message, there was a lot less boy in Tom and a lot more man. Donald had been right about him. He was doing fine. Better than fine—he was thriving on the responsibility. Making the farm *his* farm.

"*Got to go, Dad,*" his son finished up. "*Hope you're safe up there.*" He shuffled aside and Donald appeared, a little more grey, looking a little more weary. Cooper felt a twinge of guilt at having left him to shoulder so much.

"*I'm sorry, Coop,*" he said, as he had in all of the messages. "*I asked Murph to say hi, but she's as stubborn as her old man. I'll try again next time. Stay safe.*"

That was the end of it. He wondered what Murph looked like now, how twelve would lay differently from ten on her face. Would he see more of her mother there, or more of himself? Or would she look more like that part that was just Murph?

He wasn't going to find out, not this time. Maybe not ever. If she hadn't forgiven him in two years…

Sighing, he put in some ear buds and left the booth.

Romilly was in the habitat module, looking particularly pensive and unhappy. Cooper hoped his nausea hadn't returned. When it hit him, it was bad.

"You good, Rom?" he asked.

"It gets to me, Coop," Romilly admitted. "This tin can. Radiation, vacuum outside—everything wants us dead.

We're just not supposed to be here." He shook his head and looked miserable.

Cooper regarded the astrophysicist. He was the youngest member of the crew, and certainly the most highly strung. He would probably be better off behind a telescope than jetting off into space, but there weren't that many astronomers, mathematicians—scientists of any sort—left in the world. NASA poached what talent they could find from the few colleges that remained, but Cooper knew first-hand how few and rarified a group that represented. And given that kids were being taught that the American space program had been Cold War propaganda, he doubted the brain pool was getting any deeper.

No, they were lucky to have Romilly.

As long as he didn't freak out.

That had always been one of the greatest concerns regarding long-term space exploration. They'd offset the detrimental effects of prolonged weightlessness, at least to an acceptable degree. But the potential for mental deterioration could never be eliminated as a factor.

"We're explorers, Rom," he told him, trying for reassurance. "On the greatest ocean of all."

Romilly just banged his fist against the hull of the ship. The sound it made was strangely flat.

"Millimeters of aluminum—that's it," he declared. "And nothing within millions of miles that won't kill us in seconds."

He wasn't wrong there, Cooper knew. It also wasn't the point.

"A lot of the finest solo yachtsmen couldn't swim," he replied. "They knew if they fell overboard, that was it, anyway. This is no different."

Romilly seemed to chew on that without finding much to like in it. After a moment, Cooper passed him his ear buds, emitting the sounds of a thunderstorm: the pounding of the rain, the crack of lightning splitting the sky, the cricking and croaking of frogs.

"Here," he said, hoping it would relax Romilly the way it did him.

It was way too early for any of them to start losing it.

The magnificence of Saturn filled most of Cooper's field of vision, but it wasn't what held his attention. Instead he was looking over Doyle's shoulder as he parsed through a series of images. All were star fields which looked as if they had been photographed through a fish-eye lens.

"From the relay probe?" Cooper asked.

"It was in orbit around the wormhole," Doyle confirmed. "Each time it swung around, we got images of the other side of the foreign galaxy."

"Like swinging a periscope around," Cooper said.

"Exactly," Doyle replied.

"So we've got a pretty good idea what we're gonna find on the other side?" Cooper asked.

"Navigationally," Doyle said, as Brand came up from behind.

"We'll be coming up on the wormhole in less than forty-five," she said. "Suit up."

Cooper strapped into the Ranger cockpit, gazing out at the space beyond Saturn as Romilly came into the cockpit, excitement plain on his face.

Cooper keyed the radio.

"Strap in," he told the others. "I'm killing the spin."

He began firing controlled bursts from the engines, pushing against the direction of rotation. Slowly but inexorably the motion slowed, until the *Endurance* was motionless—at least relative to its own axis. And as they ground to a halt, the peculiar belly-tickle of free-fall returned.

Ahead of them, Cooper made out a distorted patch of stars, and he felt a thrill of mixed fear and wonder tremor up his spine. This was why they were here, this improbable thing.

"There!" Romilly said energetically. "That's the wormhole."

"Say it, don't spray it, Nikolai," Cooper responded, trying to keep things on an even keel. But Romilly's enthusiasm was undeterred.

"Cooper, this is a *portal*, cutting through space-time," he said. "We're seeing the heart of a galaxy so far away we don't even know where it is in the universe."

Cooper stared at the thing, the astrophysicist's words doing a slow turn in his head.

"It's a sphere," he noticed.

"Of course it is," Romilly said. "You thought it would be just a hole?"

Cooper suddenly felt like he was being called on to show his homework on the board—when he hadn't done it.

"No," he floundered. "Well, in all the illustrations..."

Romilly grabbed a piece of paper and drew two points on it, far from each other. He seemed delighted to have the opportunity to explain it all.

"In the illustrations, they're trying to show you how it works," he said, poking a hole in one of the points with his pen. "So they say, 'you wanna go from here to there, but it's too far?' A wormhole bends space like this—"

He folded the paper so the hole overlapped with the second point, then stuck his pen through both, joining them.

"—so you can take a shortcut across a higher dimension. But to show that, they've turned three-dimensional space—" He gestured around at the cockpit, then held up the paper.

"—into two dimensions. Which turns the wormhole into two dimensions… a circle."

He looked at Cooper, expecting a response.

"But what's a circle in three dimensions?" he prompted.

"A sphere," Cooper replied, suddenly getting it.

"Exactly," Romilly agreed, pointing toward their destination. "It's a spherical hole."

Cooper ruminated on that as the "spherical hole" loomed larger and larger.

"And who put it there?" Romilly continued, not ready to give it a rest. "Who do we thank?"

"I'm not thanking anyone till we get through it in one piece," Cooper replied.

"Is there any trick to this?" Cooper asked Doyle, who had replaced Romilly in the cockpit. Ahead of them, he could see the quavering stars of the other galaxy, swinging in opposition to them as they moved. It was sort of like looking into a giant shaving mirror, and it was—to say the least—disorienting.

He fired the thrusters, easing their momentum toward the thing.

"No one knows," Doyle said.

That didn't sound very reassuring.

"But the others made it, right?" he asked.

"At least some of them," Doyle replied.

Right, he thought. *Some of them.* He hadn't thought to ask how many of the Lazarus pilots hadn't sent back any signals at all, had just gone quiet after passing through the wormhole. And if it had been mentioned in one of the briefings, he must have missed it.

Or blanked it out.

"Thanks for the confidence boost," Cooper said.

He took a deep breath, then, and let it out slowly.

"Everybody ready to say goodbye to the solar system?" he asked. "To our galaxy?"

Everyone seemed to understand that it was a rhetorical question, because no one answered. So without further comment, Cooper pushed the stick forward, nosing toward the anomaly and letting gravity have them, draw them toward the center of the wormhole.

Cooper realized he was holding his breath, waiting for some sort of impact, but of course there was nothing there to hit. Instead they simply crossed into it, and suddenly the *Endurance* was part of the distortion, its warped reflection coming towards them, passing through itself.

And the universe turned inside out.

Distorted images of space-time seemed to run off in every direction, Romilly's paper bending not in three dimensions but in five, and it was happening at an ever-increasing speed, so everything was rushing by, accelerating at a dizzying pace. For the moment the *Endurance* seemed to be withstanding the elemental forces that lay beyond the hull. Cooper hoped it would stay that way.

He tried to grasp what it was his eyes were reporting. His brain told him they were racing along a sort of wall, a wall of stars and galaxies and nebulae streaking past at immense speeds. But if he shifted his gaze, it seemed more like a tunnel, albeit one that billowed out in the distance. He thought he could see an end to it, and yet that end didn't seem to be getting any closer, as if it was withdrawing from them even more quickly than they rocketed toward it.

It was the most incredible thing Cooper had ever experienced, and like nothing he ever had or could have imagined. He wasn't even sure he was going to be able to describe it later. But for now…

He looked down at his instruments. They were inert.

There was nothing there.

"They won't help you in here," Doyle said. "We're cutting through the bulk, the space beyond our three dimensions." He checked his own instruments. "All we can do is record and observe," he concluded.

Back in the ring module Brand saw a sudden apparent ripple in the air itself, which swiftly multiplied into an undulating distortion inside the ship.

Bending toward her.

Moving.

"What is that?" Romilly gasped.

It was something of a relief to know that he saw it too.

She watched the distortion come, fascinated. It didn't even occur to her to move. There was form there.

"I think…" she murmured, "I think it's *them*."

"Distorting space-time?" Romilly said.

Brand reached toward it.

"Don't!" Romilly warned, as it touched her, and her hand began to ripple; like the air, like the wormhole. But she felt nothing, no pain.

Nothing but delight.

In the Ranger, Cooper saw they were at last reaching the light at the end of the tunnel. Yet it wasn't one light, but *many*: star clusters and nebulae, galaxies and pulsars all getting closer and larger very quickly, much too quickly, impossibly fast…

And then they were out, the illusion of three dimensions snapping back into being, the rest of it folding away into the magical secret doors of the universe. It was sort of like watching a real person suddenly become a flat snapshot on paper. The image was recognizable, but depth and time—and the motion that time made possible—were all missing.

Only he didn't have the words for what was missing now, or even the concepts that the words might identify.

On the console, the instruments suddenly came back to life now that there was something for them to sense—something to which they could react.

Cooper brought his eyes up again, and stared, awestruck to his core.

"We're—here," Doyle said.

Brand's fingers were back to normal. The distortion was gone. But she kept staring at them.

"What was that?" Romilly asked her.

She touched her hand, remembering the presence, the sentience she had felt, out of phase, in different dimensions, but sharing the same space.

"The first handshake," she replied.

SEVENTEEN

Earth's sun was nowhere near the center of its galaxy, but was in a hinterland nearer the edge of it, where the stars were thin and distant from one another—a lonely house on a great plain.

Certainly not a condo in the city.

This place, this sky beyond the wormhole, this was more like New York. Or Chicago, at least. Stars blazed everywhere, some brightly enough to leave impressions on Cooper's retinas. Gauzy nebulae draped between and among them, coloring whole quadrants of space with light refracted through gas and dust and the fresh brilliance of newly born stars.

From Earth, the only nebulae you could see with the naked eye were tiny dull smudges that looked like blurry stars. Here they hove up like thunderheads.

If their new home was indeed going to be here, it would have a much more interesting night sky. Probably a more interesting day sky, if it came to that.

I'm in another galaxy, he thought, trying to really grasp what had just happened. The closest star to Earth was so far away a light wave would take four years to travel between them. The nearest galaxy to Earth was two-and-a-half million light years away. Two-and-a-half million years for light to make the trip. This galaxy—this one could be *anywhere*.

If he had a telescope powerful enough to see home from here, he wouldn't see his kids. Dinosaurs, maybe. Or trilobites. Or a cooling fireball. Or nothing, if he was more than five billion light years from Earth. Which he could easily be. According to Romilly, folding space a trillion light years would yield no longer a journey than folding it ten miles. But the distance after the fold—

That was real.

So to reach the planets on their itinerary, they still had to make their way through a lot of vacuum.

Far from home didn't begin to describe how he felt in that moment.

Doyle studied his workstation. The initial maneuvering done, they were all back in the ring module, processing both their feelings and the data that was pouring in.

"The lost communications came through," Doyle informed them.

"How?" Brand asked.

"The relay on this side cached them," he explained, as he continued to parse through it.

"Years of basic data," he added. "No real surprises. Miller's site has kept pinging thumbs up, as has Mann's… but Edmunds went down three years ago."

"Transmitter failure?" Brand asked. Cooper heard the anxiety in her voice, and felt a little sorry for her.

"Maybe," Doyle replied. "He was sending the thumbs up right till it went dark."

"Miller still looks good?" Romilly asked.

As Doyle affirmed that, the astrophysicist began

drawing a great big circle on a whiteboard.

"She's coming up fast," he said. "With one complication. The planet is much closer to Gargantua than we expected."

"Gargantua?" Cooper said, not sure he liked the sound of it.

"A very large black hole," Doyle explained. "Miller's and Dr. Mann's planets orbit it."

Brand looked at the diagram Romilly was working on. If the big circle was the circumference of Gargantua, then the orbit he was tracing was pretty much the same.

"And Miller's is on the horizon?" Brand said.

"A basketball around the hoop," Romilly confirmed. "Landing there takes us dangerously close. A black hole that big has a huge gravitational pull."

Cooper studied their grave faces, wondering why they were so concerned. It seemed easy enough for them to compensate.

"Look," he said, "I can swing around that neutron star to decelerate—"

Brand cut him off.

"It's not that," she said. "It's *time*. That gravity will slow our clock, compared to Earth's. Drastically."

Cooper suddenly understood their expressions. Black holes did crazy things with time. He'd even mentioned that to Murph—but he had never believed it would actually be an issue he'd need to address.

As in many things, he had been wrong.

"How bad?" he asked, thinking that he most likely didn't want to know.

"Every hour we spend on that planet will be maybe…" She did the mental computations. "Seven years back on Earth."

"Jesus…" Cooper breathed.

"That's relativity, folks," Romilly said.

Cooper felt as if the floor had been pulled out from beneath his feet. All of a sudden Miller's world seemed a helluva lot less hospitable.

"We can't drop down there without considering the consequences," he said.

"Cooper, we have a mission," Doyle said.

"That's easy for you to say," Cooper returned. "You don't have anyone back on Earth waiting for you, do you?"

"You have no idea what's easy for me," Doyle shot back, frowning.

Brand actually came to his aid, for once.

"Cooper's right," she said. "We have to think of time as a resource, just like oxygen and food. Going down there is going to cost us."

Doyle relented, and stepped to the screen, a determined look on his face.

"Look," he said. "Dr. Mann's data looks promising, but we won't get there for months. Edmunds' is even further. Miller hasn't sent much, but what she *has* sent is promising—water, organics."

"You don't find that every day," Brand conceded.

"No, you do not," Doyle agreed, his blue eyes flaring. "So think about the resources it would take to come *back* here…"

Yeah, Cooper granted. *He's got a point.* In essence, getting from Miller's planet to Mann's would require climbing out of the deep gravitational well of Gargantua. It would be like swimming upstream, against the current. Which probably wouldn't leave enough fuel for a return trip to Earth. If the choice was between getting back a little late and not getting back at all, he knew where he fell out.

"How far back from the planet would we have to stay to be out of the time shift?" Cooper asked.

Romilly pointed to his whiteboard drawing of the

massive black hole and the planet skimming just above its horizon.

"Just back from the cusp," he said.

"So we track a wider orbit of Gargantua," Cooper said. "Parallel with Miller's planet but a little further out... Take a Ranger down, grab Miller and her samples, debrief, and analyze back here."

"That'll work," Brand said.

"No time for monkey business or chitchat down there," Cooper emphasized. "Tars, you'd better wait up here. Who else?'

Romilly lifted his head.

"If we're talking about a couple of years—I'd use that time to work on gravity—observations from the wormhole," he said. "This is gold to Professor Brand."

A *couple of years*, Cooper thought. He glanced at Romilly, and wondered if the man really understood what he was saying. He would be here—alone—for *years*. Of the four of them, Romilly had proven the least comfortable in space, the most susceptible to its physical and psychological perils.

Yet he would also be the least useful on the surface, and the most useful up here.

It felt like a huge decision to make in so little time, and not just because of Romilly.

Like Brand said, though, time was as much a resource to them as air. It wasn't just seeing his kids again. If they lost too much time, there would be no human race to save, except for the embryos they'd brought with them. End result: no plan A.

And he was determined that there would be a plan A, come hell or high water.

"Okay," he said. "Tars, factor an orbit of Gargantua—minimal thrusting, conserve fuel—but stay in range."

"Don't worry," Tars said. "I wouldn't leave you

behind…" Abruptly he turned away from Cooper. "…Dr. Brand," he finished, with a comic's timing.

Cooper wondered if it might be a good idea to bring the robot's humor setting down another notch or two.

Amelia Brand considered the black hole.

If the wormhole was a three-dimensional hole you could see through—albeit in a distorted fashion—Gargantua was a three-dimensional hole into *nothing*.

The average black hole had in some distant past been a star, and probably a really big one, merrily fusing hydrogen into helium, pushing enough energy out to keep its own gravity from making it collapse. But eventually, over billions of years, the hydrogen had all burned out, and it had to start using helium for fuel. And when the helium was all gone, it turned to progressively heavier and heavier elements.

Until one day it lost its fight with the gravity it had itself created. The force keeping it shining and inflated wasn't enough to counter its mass. So it collapsed, victorious gravity crushing its atoms into denser and denser substances until finally crushing the atoms themselves in neutrons. The physical size of the star became less and less, but its gravity grew exponentially. In the end, even light couldn't escape its pull, but it could still grow, swallowing nebulae, planets, stars.

Yet Gargantua was anything but "average." Formed when the universe was young, perhaps at the center of a galaxy, it may have been the product of many smaller black holes, merging until its mass was at least a hundred million times that of the Earth's sun.

Present-day Gargantua was frightening in its seeming nothingness. Yet past its horizon, past the point of no return, beyond which even light could not come back, Amelia could see an effect—a glowing disk surrounded the black hole, gas and particles captured by the immense gravity, whirling around it like water going down a spherical drain. So incredibly fast was the spin that the atoms collided with one another, hurling bursts of energy into the cloud, quickening it with light and blowing like a wind back out through the disk, creating plasma arabesques of breathtaking beauty.

But deeper, where that eldritch, glowing shroud met the Gargantua's event horizon… was a horrifying nothingness.

"A literal heart of darkness," Doyle said.

That didn't seem sufficient to Amelia—as if the man was damning Gargantua with faint praise. She pointed, drawing his gaze from the terrifying naught of the black hole to a small, glowing point.

"That's Miller's planet," she said.

Cooper turned to Case, the robot, who was riding shotgun in the copilot's seat.

"Ready?" he asked.

"Yup," the robot replied.

"Don't say much, do you?" Cooper said wryly.

"Tars talks plenty for both of us," Case said.

Cooper chuckled, and threw a switch.

"Detach," he said. Then he watched as the ring module seemed to drift away from them, and felt a moment's hesitation.

Then Gargantua took hold of them, and they were suddenly streaking away from *Endurance*, ridiculously fast.

"Romilly, you reading these forces?" he asked, not quite believing what he was seeing.

"*Unbelievable*" Romilly's words crackled over the radio, but even from this distance, Cooper could hear the excitement in his voice. "*If we could see the collapsed star inside, the singularity, we'd solve gravity."*

Cooper gazed down at the gaping black wound in the universe.

"No way to get anything from it?" he asked.

"Nothing escapes the horizon," Romilly replied. *"Not even light. The answer's there, there's just no way to see it."*

Cooper fastened his attention on the blue marble skimming along Gargantua's event horizon, because it was coming up fast. He ran the trajectory one more time.

"This is fast for atmospheric entry," Case noticed. "Should we use the thrusters to slow?"

"We're gonna use the Ranger's aerodynamics to save fuel," Cooper told the machine.

"Airbrake?" Case said. Cooper noted for future reference that Case apparently had an "are you *kidding* me?" setting.

"Wanna get in fast, don't we?" he replied.

"Brand, Doyle, get ready," Case said. A robot couldn't be nervous, Cooper knew, but somehow this one sounded anxious.

He watched the planet below. From a distance it hadn't looked so different from Earth, but as they drew closer, he could see that it was much—well—*bluer.* He tried to pick out features—continents, islands—but all he could make out were clouds.

Then they reached the outskirts of the atmosphere and he didn't have any attention to spare.

It started like a whisper, air so thin it would pass as vacuum compared to sea-level air on Earth. But at the speed they were traveling, those few molecules were compressed enough to make them practically much denser in their interaction with the plummeting vessel. That was good, actually, because this way they could ease into the atmosphere.

Well, maybe not ease, he thought, as the ship began to shudder and the air outside shrieked in protest. The Ranger's nose began to glow as the friction from the atmosphere mounted, and every weld in the craft seemed to object as he tried to flatten out their course a bit, to engage the atmosphere like a jet, rather than a meteorite.

Cooper glanced at his instruments, and then back at the horizon.

"We could ease—" Case began.

"Hands where I can see them, Case!" Cooper shouted. "Only time I ever went down was a machine easing at the wrong moment."

"A little caution," Case pleaded.

"Can get you killed, same as recklessness," Cooper opined.

"Cooper!" Doyle chimed in. "Too damned fast!"

"I got this," Cooper said, as the ship threatened to shake apart around them His knuckles on the controls were white as he tried to keep them from vibrating out of his hands.

"Should I disable feedback?" Case asked.

"No!" Cooper exploded. "No, I need to feel the air..."

The lander was white-hot now, cutting through a layer of clouds as thin as razors.

"Do we have a fix on the beacon?" he asked.

"Got it!" Case said. "Can you maneuver?"

Yeah, he thought. *We have our choice of crash sites, as long as most of them are more-or-less straight down.*

"Gotta shave more speed," he said instead. "I'll try and spiral down to it."

A moment later they burst through the clouds. The surface looked far too close to Cooper, but at least they seemed to be over a level surface...

"Just water," Doyle said.

Cooper realized he was right. They were over an ocean.

"The stuff of life…" Brand said.

"Twelve hundred meters out," Case advised.

Cooper banked as hard as he could, trying to shed more speed. The surface was coming fast.

"It's shallow," Brand said. "Feet deep…"

Now they were low enough they were kicking up a splash, like an overgrown speedboat.

"Seven hundred meters," Case intoned.

Cooper watched the water sheeting toward him.

"Wait for it…" he said.

"Five hundred meters."

Cooper yanked the stick back.

"Fire!" he said.

The retro-rockets kicked in just above the surface, punching back against their velocity. He tried to hold it, but the craft slewed sideways as the landing gear came down. They dropped, hit the water, casting up a spray. The impact nearly jarred Cooper's teeth loose, but he held on stubbornly. Then when the air cleared, they were down, and everything looked good. Brand had been right—the water was really, really shallow—so much so that the landing gear held the Ranger just above the surface.

"Very graceful," Brand managed. Cooper noticed she and Doyle were staring at him. Both of them looked a little roughed up.

"No," he said. "But it was very *efficient*."

They still just stared, but he pretty much ignored it, wondering how much time had already passed on Earth.

Days?

Months?

Better not to think about it, he decided.

"What're you waiting for?" he barked. "Go!"

They snapped out of it then, unfastening their harnesses, checking their helmets. Case detached himself from the floor and went to the hatch. It cracked open, and light and spray blew into the cabin.

It caught Cocper, then, in his gut—they were on another world.

EIGHTEEN

Amelia followed Doyle and Case into the shallow sea. Cooper remained aboard the Ranger.

She experimented with sloshing through it as Case took a moment to orient himself. The water felt thicker, heavier than it should. More viscous. It might have been the bulk of her spacesuit, but she didn't think so. They had practiced with those underwater, back on Earth, in preparation for the mission.

Here, though, it was different.

"This way," Case directed. "About two hundred meters."

Amelia looked in the direction the robot indicated. The water stretched out to the horizon, where it met a mountain range, misty with distance; one long ridge that vanished in each direction. The sight of the alien skyline arrested her for a moment, and she wished they weren't in such a hurry. She had long dreamt of her first moments on an extra-solar planet, and this wasn't how it was supposed to go. There should be a little ceremony, a little "That's one small step."

Instead they were in this tearing hurry, and it felt completely half-assed. But it was what it was. They weren't here to set up flags and take pictures.

So she pushed forward.

Spacesuits, she decided after a few feet, were not well designed for wading. They were heavy, clumsy, and didn't give one much of a feel for the surface on which one was walking. And that wasn't the only thing making it difficult to make any progress.

"The gravity's punishing," Doyle panted.

"Floating around in space too long?" Amelia teased.

"One hundred and thirty percent Earth gravity," Case informed them.

Right, Amelia thought. That explained a lot. This much more gravity wasn't ideal, but it was something people couldn adapt to. Water was a good sign, and with any luck, there would be at least some habitable land at the foot of the mountains...

They pushed on, with Case still in the lead and Doyle falling behind.

After what seemed like an eternity, Case stopped.

"Should be here," he said, and with that he began moving in a search pattern. Amelia moved to join him.

"The signal's coming from here," she said, but as soon as she spoke, it didn't make any sense. The beacon should be with the ship, yet the ship clearly wasn't here. Even if Miller had crashed, the water here wasn't deep enough to hide the wreck.

Where had it gone?

Suddenly Case dropped down and began thrashing under the water. He looked for all the world like a film Amelia had once seen, of a bear fishing in a river. That is, if a bear were rectangular, and had metal instead of fur on its exterior.

* ✳ *

Cooper watched Brand, Doyle, and Case with mounting unease. He could almost feel the clock in his head ticking off the time passing back on Earth. How could humanity hope to live on a world so hopelessly out of synch with the rest of the universe?

His chest began to tighten, and he took deep breaths, trying to settle himself. He stared off at the mountains. Something about them reminded him of home, but he couldn't quite figure out why. He remembered driving toward the mountains with Murph, watching them grow larger as he followed the directions left by "them" on Murph's floor.

But that wasn't it. The mountains that hid the old NORAD facility were relatively young peaks; jagged, snowcapped. These formed a startlingly uniform ridge, like a long fold in the planet's crust. And as tall as they seemed, he couldn't make out a snowline, unless it was at the very top—that thin little film of white.

Then he realized—it wasn't mountains he was reminded of at all. Instead, he thought of a dust storm in the distance, a black wall churning across the land.

Doyle finally caught up with them, thoroughly out of breath.

"What is he doing?" Doyle asked, nodding at the mechanical.

Case answered him by pulling something up from the seabed—if that was what it could be called. Silt streaming off of it suggested that it had been at least partially buried.

"Her beacon," Amelia said, heart sinking. Where was Miller?

Case dutifully began carrying the beacon toward the Ranger.

"Wreckage," Doyle said, echoing her own thoughts. "Where's the rest?"

But she was ahead of him—she had already spotted some flotsam.

"Toward the mountains!" she said, and she starting slogging that way as quickly as she could.

Cooper's voice crackled over the radio.

"Those aren't mountains," he said. His voice sounded strange. She paused and looked at the range again. Did they seem a little more distant?

It had to be some sort of optical illusion.

"They're waves…" Cooper's disembodied voice told her.

That went through her like an electrical shock. Not waves, but *a* wave… one unbelievably huge wave. She could see the tiny white line of foam at the top of it. How high was it? A mile? More? Perspective made it impossible to tell.

It was moving away from them, thank God.

She had to get the recorder. It had to be here. She plowed through the water toward the wreckage.

Cooper heard some bumping below as Case loaded the beacon. He watched the monster wave recede and then, a peculiar feeling in his gut, he turned to look in the direction it had come from.

And saw the next one looming over them, blotting out the sky.

"Brand, get back here!" he shouted frantically into the comm.

"We need the recorder," she protested.

Before he could say anything, Doyle's voice sputtered over the radio.

"Case," Doyle shouted. *"Go get her!"*

Cooper slammed his fist into the dash.

What the hell is Brand doing?

"Dammit!" he yelled. "Brand, get back here!"

But she was still out there, looking through the junk in the water.

"We can't leave without her data," Brand insisted.

"You don't have time!" he replied.

He saw Case pass Doyle, who was headed back toward the Ranger, struggling against water and gravity.

"Go, go!" Doyle yelled at the robot.

Case blew past him, churning a wake as he made a beeline toward Brand, reconfigured in wheel-like form.

Cooper ran to the hatch and swung it open. In the distance, he saw Brand trying to lift something out of the water. He looked back at the approaching wave, knowing that it must be thousands of feet high, trying to judge how close it was, how fast it was moving, but the scale made it difficult for his mind to comprehend.

"Get back here, now!" he hollered.

Brand pulled something up. He couldn't see what it was, but after a moment of struggle she slipped and fell backward. Whatever it was came down on top of her.

She didn't get back up, although he could see her arms moving. Her face turned toward him, and even at that distance he saw it turn up, focused on the mountain of water hurtling toward them.

"Cooper, go!" she yelled. *"Go! I can't make it."*

"Get up, Brand!" he commanded.

"Go! Get out of here!"

But then Case was there. He flipped the junk away from her, heaved her onto his back, and raced back toward the Ranger.

That's when Cooper noticed Doyle, just standing there, transfixed by the impossible wave.

"Doyle!" he shouted. "Come on! Case has her!"

The man shook it off and started running back as best he could, struggling with every step.

Cooper jumped back up into the cockpit and started powering up. All he could see now was the wave.

"Come on, come on…" he muttered. Time was almost up.

Desperate, he ran back to the hatch. Doyle had made it to the foot of the ladder, and Case was arriving with Brand. Puffing, Doyle stepped aside to make way for the robot and its passenger.

"Go!" Doyle said.

Case obediently pushed past him, jerking himself up the ladder and unceremoniously dumping Brand inside the ship. Then he turned to help Doyle, who was struggling to ascend the ladder himself.

Before he could get there, the Ranger suddenly jumped up as the leading edge of the surge heaved them out of the shallow trough and up the side of the wave. The Ranger tilted sharply and seawater slapped Doyle back, out of Case's grip, as it came raging across the hatch. The ship was lifted and everything went sideways.

That fast—the blink of an eye—Doyle was gone.

For that second, Cooper was without emotion. He saw Doyle swept away and knew with crystalline certainty that there was absolutely nothing he could do. Nothing but try to save himself and the others.

"Shut the hatch!" he told Case.

Case obeyed as Cooper stumbled across the tilting deck back to the controls.

"Power down! Power down!" he said. "We have to ride it out." Emotion returned in a rush. He felt like a coward for abandoning Doyle, although he still understood it would have meant the end of all of them to keep the hatch open. But mostly he felt simple, unadorned fury.

And he turned it on Brand.

"We were *not* prepared for this!" he shouted.

They were already hundreds of feet in the air, sucked sideways up the mountain of water, and Cooper found himself tossed like a doll across the cockpit as the Ranger began to roll. He managed to grab Brand and jam her into her seat, and after that it was all he could do not to vomit or lose consciousness as everything turned around him.

It was like the Straights all over again; all control gone, at the mercy of the universe...

NINETEEN

After an eternity, the craft stopped rolling and settled upright. Cooper scrambled into his seat as water poured away from the canopy, and he could see their surroundings.

They were at the top of the wave. A glance at his instruments told him they were an absurd four freaking thousand feet above the surface. For a moment, the Ranger surfed along the foaming back of the leviathan, and the view was unreal. The papery clouds above, the sea stretching out in all directions, impossibly far below them, the distant back of the last wave on the horizon, a faint line of white in the other direction.

Cooper stared past the powered-down controls at the incredible fall they were about to take.

Then they took it. Once again he felt free-fall, but this time he knew there would be a stop at the end of it.

It was all a jumble of pain, terror, and near-absolute disorientation, and it seemed to last forever.

* ✳ *

When the craft finally came to rest, Cooper groggily lurched to the control panel, his hands flying over the controls, powering up. Miraculously, everything came on, so he wasted no time in starting the engines.

They coughed. They sputtered. But they wouldn't start. *Of course.*

He felt the landing gear lift them out the water, and tried the engines again.

Still nothing.

"Too waterlogged," Case said. "Let it drain."

"Goddamn!" Cooper shouted, hammering the console.

"I told you to leave me," Brand said.

"And I told you to get your ass back here," he retorted. "Difference is, only one of us was thinking about the mission."

"Cooper, you were thinking about getting home," she countered. "I was trying to do the right thing!"

"Tell that to Doyle," he shot back.

The hurt registered in her eyes, and he was glad. He looked at the clock.

"How long to drain, Case?" he asked.

"Forty-five to an hour," the robot informed him.

Cooper shook his head and uncoupled his helmet. The cabin was pressurized. Everything smelled wet, but it didn't smell like seawater or a pond. It smelled like distilled water that had been dumped on hot rocks—a mineral scent, but not salt.

"The stuff of life, huh?" he said. "What's this gonna cost us, Brand?"

"A lot," she said. "Decades." Her voice was flat.

Cooper felt like he couldn't breathe. *Decades.* Tom and Murph were adults already. How old? It seemed impossible. He rubbed his face, trying to comprehend it. He watched the wave go, knowing there would be another, and soon.

He tried to return his focus to the mission.

"What happened to Miller?" he asked.

"Judging by the wreckage," Brand said, "she was broken up by a wave soon after impact."

"How could the wreckage still be here after all these years?" he wondered aloud.

"Because of the time slippage," Brand said. "On this planet's time, she landed here just hours ago. She might have only died minutes ago."

Case indicated the beacon, back by the airlock.

"The data Doyle received was just the initial status, echoing endlessly," the machine said.

Cooper felt his throat closing.

"We're not prepared for this, Brand," he said. "You're a bunch of eggheads without the survival skills of a Boy Scout troop."

"We got this far on our brains," she said defensively. "Further than any humans in history."

"Not far enough," he said. "And we're stuck here till there won't be anyone left on Earth to save."

"I'm counting every second, same as you, Cooper," she said.

He digested that silently for a while. He wasn't the only one who had left someone behind. Was her father even still alive? How old had he been when they left? And then there was Edmunds, maybe waiting out there, waiting for her to come rescue him.

"Do you have some way we can jump into a black hole and get back the years?" he finally asked.

She dismissed that with a wag of her head.

"Don't just shake your head at me!" he snapped.

"Time is relative," Brand said. "It can stretch and squeeze—but it can't run backward. The only thing that can move across the dimensions like time is gravity."

He knew that. He'd read it. But he wasn't ready to give up. Brand didn't know everything—that much was abundantly clear.

"The beings that led us here," he said. "They communicate through gravity. Could they be talking to us from the future?"

She was silent for a moment.

"Maybe," she said at last.

"Well if *they* can—"

Brand cut him off.

"Look, Cooper," she said, "they're creatures of at least five dimensions. To *them* the past might be a canyon they can climb into, and the future a mountain they can climb up. But to us it's not. Okay?"

She took off her helmet and regarded him frankly.

"I'm sorry, Cooper," she said. "I screwed up. But you knew about relativity."

"My daughter was ten," he said bitterly. "I couldn't explain Einstein's theories before I left."

"Couldn't you tell her you were going to save the world?" Brand asked.

"No," he said. "As a parent, I understood the most important thing—let your kids feel safe. Which rules out telling a ten-year-old that the world's ending."

"Cooper?" Case said urgently.

He looked, although he already knew what it had to be. And it was—another wave.

They had been more than lucky to survive the first one. He didn't place great odds on making it through two. Even if they did, they would be waterlogged again, and have to wait another couple of decades.

Now or never.

"How long for the engines?" he asked.

"A minute or two," Case replied.

"We don't have it," Cooper snapped. He tried the engines again as the wave loomed over them. They coughed and blew out steam. But that was all.

He tried again.

Nothing.

And again.

"Helmets on!" he said, as the wave came upon them.

TWENTY

Cooper felt the ship lifting as the water began to climb. His mind ran desperately through the vessel's systems, capabilities.

There had to be an answer...

Maybe there was.

"Blow our cabin oxygen through the main thrusters," he told Case. "We'll spark it."

The robot didn't waste any time. There was an immediate shriek of air leaving the cabin, sucked toward the engines.

Brand barely got her helmet on in time.

"Come on, now," Cooper said, taking a run at the engines again. *We've only got one more shot.*

This time the engines blasted to life, blowing the Ranger clear of the wave and up toward the beckoning sky, but the wave wasn't ready to give them up. He watched the wall of water, heart hammering. But then they really kicked in, and the craft brushed past the monstrous crest, and they were beyond it, free.

In his last glimpse of the surface, Cooper thought he saw Doyle's lifeless body lying in the shallows, but then the wave eclipsed his view.

He turned the Ranger skyward and pushed.

When Romilly met them as they entered the ring module, his appearance hit Amelia almost like a physical shock. She thought she was prepared.

She was wrong.

His beard now had gray in it. Wrinkles had developed around his eyes, and there was a lost look in those eyes, as if he didn't quite believe they were really there—as if he were seeing ghosts.

"Hello, Rom," she said.

"I've waited years," Romilly said.

"How many years?" Cooper asked, a little harshly.

Romilly looked thoughtful.

"By now it must be—"

"Twenty-three years…" Tars provided.

Cooper's head dropped.

"…four months, eight days," Tars finished.

Cooper turned away from them.

"Doyle?" Romilly asked.

Amelia found she couldn't meet Romilly's eyes, but she shook her head. Then she forced her gaze back up, and grasped his hands.

"I thought I was prepared," she told him. "I knew all the theory." She paused, gathered her words. "The reality is different."

"And Miller?" Romilly asked.

"There's nothing here for us," she told him.

She studied his aged face. Then a thought struck her.

"Why didn't you sleep?" she asked.

"I did, a couple of stretches," he said. "But I stopped believing you were coming back, and something seems wrong about dreaming your life away."

He smiled faintly.

"I learned what I could from studying the black hole," he went on, "but I couldn't send anything to your father. We've been receiving, but nothing gets out."

Twenty-three years, she thought. That would make her father...

"Is he still alive?" she asked.

To her relief, Romilly nodded. She closed her eyes.

"We've got years of messages stored," Romilly said.

Amelia opened her eyes and saw that Cooper was ahead of her, settling into the booth.

Cooper sat staring at the comm for what seemed a long time before he worked up the nerve to turn it on.

"Cooper," he finally said.

"*Messages span twenty-three years,*" the automated voice announced.

"I know," he whispered. "Just start at the beginning." The screen came to life, and there was Tom, just as he had looked in the last message, still seventeen.

"*Hi, Dad—*" Tom began.

With trembling fingers, Cooper paused the playback and took a breath, trying to steel himself.

Then he let it run.

"*I met another girl, Dad,*" Tom said. "*I really think this is the one.*" He held up a picture of himself and a teenaged girl, dark hair, dark eyes—she was pretty.

"*Murph stole Grandpa's car,*" he went on. "*She crashed it. She's okay, though. Your truck's still running. Grandpa said she would steal that the next time. I said if she did it'd be the last thing she did...*"

Cooper leaned back and just let it come, tears streaming

down his face. And it kept coming for a long time, and he kept hoping that maybe, maybe Murph would appear. But she didn't. It was always Tom or Donald. So he watched them age.

He wasn't sure how long he had been sitting there, but Tom was talking again. He looked twenty-something now.

"I've got a surprise for you, Dad," he said. *"You're a grandpa."*

He held up a tiny, squinty-eyed infant, tightly swaddled.

"Congratulations," Tom said. *"Meet Jesse."*

Cooper smiled, feeling his eyes fill with tears. Knowing that the baby he was looking at now wasn't a baby anymore.

His grandson…

"I wanted to name him Coop, but Lois said maybe the next one. Grandpa said he already had the 'great' part," Tom went on, *"so we just leave it at that…"*

The screen cut again, then came back to life. Tom again, maybe a decade older. The boy was gone completely. What Cooper saw now was a weary man holding a lot of weight on his shoulders.

"Hi, Dad," Tom said. *"I'm sorry it's been a while. What with Jesse and all…"*

He paused, a sorrowful expression on his face, and Cooper realized something must have happened to the baby. His grandson. How long had he lived? What had he been like?

"Grandpa died last week," Tom continued. *"We buried him out in the back forty, next to Mom and Jesse."* He looked down. *"Where we'd have buried you, if you'd ever come back."* His gaze returned to the camera. *"Murph was there for the funeral,"* he said. *"I don't see her so much anymore."*

Tom sighed, and his face settled into lines of resignation.

"You're not listening to this," he said. "I know that. All these messages are just out there, drifting in the darkness. I figured as long as they were willing to send them, there was some hope, but... you're gone. You're never coming back. I've known that for a long time. Lois says—that's my wife, Dad—she says I have to let you go. So I am."

He looked as if he wanted to say something more, then apparently he decided against it.

Cooper started to reach toward the screen, as if somehow he could ask Tom to stay, to tell him he was alive.

But he couldn't.

On the screen, Tom reached his hand toward the camera.

"Wherever you are," Tom said, "I hope you're at peace.

"Goodbye, Dad."

The screen went black, but Cooper kept looking at it, wiping the tears from his face, his heart like lead.

Goodbye, Donald, he thought. It was hard to believe Donald was dead. He'd been such a sturdy presence, so much a part of that place. And Cooper had put so much on him—first forcing him to pick up much of what Erin had left when she died, and then the kids themselves. And he had taken the load, quietly—with some commentary, but no real complaint. Not really, all things considered.

He owed the old man a lot, and there was no way to repay him.

Sometimes you have to see your life from far away for it to make sense, he thought. To see what was probably obvious to anyone else.

Goodbye, Tom, he said silently. Goodbye, son...

Of course Murph couldn't forgive him. Her mother had left her forever, but her mother hadn't any choice about it. Then her father had left, too. But her father chose to leave her. How could she forgive that?

How could he have not seen it? It had been right in front of him.

Like so many things.

The screen was still dark—the recordings were done. He couldn't help but touch the screen, his only connection to his family.

And then the screen flashed back on. He pulled his hand back in surprise.

There was a woman looking at him, late thirties, early forties, flaming red hair. Beautiful. She started to say something, and then stopped, looking unsure. Then her eyes settled into a determined expression. It was shockingly familiar.

"*Hello, Dad,*" she finally said. "*You sonofabitch.*"

Cooper's eyes widened.

"Murph?" he whispered.

"*I never made one of these when you were still responding, 'cos I was so mad at you for leaving. When you went quiet, it seemed like I should just live with my decision.*" She paused, then added, "*And I have...*

"*But today's my birthday,*" she explained. "*And it's a special one because you once told me—*"

Her voice caught, and for a moment she couldn't speak.

"*You once told me that when you came back we might be the same age... and today I'm the same age you were when you left.*" Her eyes glistened as tears started to form.

"*So it'd be a real good time for you to come back,*" she said.

Then she switched off the camera.

Again, Cooper stared at the empty screen.

Happy birthday, Murph, he thought, stunned.

What have I done?

TWENTY-ONE

"I didn't mean to intrude," a voice said softly, as Murph wiped her tears. She turned and found Professor Brand there. She hadn't heard his wheelchair approach.

"I've never seen you in here before," he said.

Murph stood up.

"I've never been in here before," she said. Without really thinking, she took the handles on the back of the wheelchair and began to conduct him into the corridor.

She'd thought he would never surrender to the chair — he'd tried to make do with canes and crutches at first, which led to more falls, one of them life-threatening. At some point she had managed to make him see that he could do what was really important to him sitting down, as well as standing — probably better.

"I talk to Amelia all of the time," the professor said. "It helps. I'm glad you've started."

"I haven't," Murph replied. "I just had something I wanted to get out."

If he'd asked her, she might have gone further, but she might not have. And he didn't ask — she knew he wouldn't. Professor Brand had been part of her life for a long time.

He'd pulled her out of school, brought her here to be educated, taken her under his wing. Given her something real to do.

Her father had been around for ten years of her life. The professor had been an everyday part of her existence for almost three times that long. She loved him, in a way, and he would probably say the same thing about her. But he respected the hard, secret core of her. He never tried to push into the thoughts and feelings onto which she put the strongest guards, and she in turn respected his silences, as well.

He spoke of Amelia often enough that Murph almost felt she knew her, even though they had only met the once, long ago. But as often as the professor brought her up, there was something he never admitted. Something Murph knew intuitively.

He believed he would never see his daughter again.

With that, she could empathize. It was a bond that held them together, this unspoken fear.

They reached the professor's office a few moments later. He wheeled himself behind his desk.

"I know they're still out there," he said.

"I know," Murph replied. She wasn't so sure herself, but the professor needed her encouragement.

"There are so many reasons their communications might not be getting through."

"I know, Professor," she said.

"I'm not sure which I'm more afraid of," he went on. "They never come back, or they come back to find we've failed."

"Then let's succeed," Murph said.

He's looking old, she thought. *Weary. And—something else*. Something she couldn't place.

The professor pressed his lips together and nodded. He

pointed at the formula that filled much of his office.

"So," he began, "back from the fourth iteration, let's run it with a finite set."

Murph paused as she picked up her notebook.

Really?

"With respect, Professor," she said, "we've tried that a hundred times."

"And it only has to work *once*, Murph," he replied.

She shrugged, and reluctantly began following his instructions.

Later, they sat on a walkway eating sandwiches and watching the continuing construction on the big ship. As his eyes wandered over the gigantic cylinder, she saw the pride on Professor Brand's face, and it felt like old times, like when he'd first brought her here after her father left. When she'd first begun to learn about the mission, and to believe. To understand the purpose of her life.

"Every rivet they drive in could have been a bullet," he said. "We've done well for the world, here. Whether or not we crack the equation before I kick—"

"Don't be morbid, Professor," Murph chided. She did it lightly, but the fact was that the professor's death was something she really didn't want to think about. Almost everyone important to her was dead, or might as well be. There were only Professor Brand and Tom, and she and Tom—well, there was something broken there.

"I'm not afraid of death, Murph," the professor told her. "I'm an old physicist. I'm afraid of *time*."

That tickled something in the back of her brain, but it wasn't until after lunch, when they were back in his office, that it went from tickle to scratch, then to an epiphanic whack on the head.

"Time," she said. "You're afraid of time…"

She was sure, now.

"Professor," she said, "the equation…?"

He looked up from his work. She took a deep breath, and plunged on.

"For years we've tried to solve it without changing the underlying assumptions about time," she said.

"And?" he replied mildly.

"And that means each iteration becomes an attempt to prove its own proof. It's recursive. Nonsensical—"

"Are you calling my life's work 'nonsense,' Murph?" he snapped irritably.

"No," she replied, feeling unaccountably a little angry herself. "I'm saying you've been trying to solve it with one arm—no, with *both* arms tied behind your back."

She suddenly felt, not uncertain but… wary.

"And I don't understand *why*," she finished.

Professor Brand gazed at the floor, then started wheeling his chair away.

"I'm an old man, Murph," he said. "Could we pick this up another time? I'd like to talk to my daughter."

She nodded, watching him go, wondering what the hell was going on.

Amelia Brand watched her father age before her eyes. He talked about the mission, asked how she was, made note of minor aches and pains, and filled her in on the people she might remember. Someone named Getty had become a medical doctor. At first she didn't know who he meant, because the Gettys she remembered had both been cyberneticists—until she remembered that they'd had a son, ten or twelve years old when she left.

She had been his babysitter, once or twice.

He told her that he had a bright new assistant: Cooper's daughter. The girl, Murph, was working with him on the gravity equation, and he seemed confident that they nearly had it solved.

As the years passed, he continued to be optimistic. She kept hoping that in the next message he would declare "Eureka!" but in the course of messages that spanned more than two decades, it never happened. Still, plan A was proceeding apace, he assured her. The first of the huge ship-stations was nearing completion, awaiting only something to lift it free of the tyranny of planetary gravity.

He never said anything about it, but at some point she realized he was in a wheelchair, and it was probably permanent. And yet, even as frail as he appeared, she could still hear the passion in his voice, see it in his eyes. He had not bowed to time, and he didn't expect anyone else to do so.

"Stepping out into the universe," he told her toward the end, eyes watery but alert, "we must first confront the reality that nothing in our solar system can help us. Then we must confront the realities of interstellar travel. We must venture far beyond the reach of our own life spans, must think not as individuals, but as a species…"

TWENTY-TWO

Cooper nodded as Brand joined them. It was time to decide what to do next, to stop licking their wounds and move on.

"Tars kept *Endurance* right where we needed her," Cooper said. "But it took years longer than we anticipated..."

An orbit was a controlled fall, really, and most weren't stable over time. That had been known as far back as Newton, who spent gallons of ink trying to figure out why the planets hadn't tumbled into the sun or spun off into space. In the end his best guess was that God just didn't want it that way, so now and then He would toss a comet through the solar system to put everything back on track.

He put up the images of the remaining planets: Mann's white dot and Edmunds' red one.

"We don't have the fuel to visit both prospects," he said. "We have to choose."

"How?" Romilly asked. "They're both promising. Edmunds' data was better, but Dr. Mann is the one still transmitting."

"We have no reason to suppose Edmunds' results would have soured," Brand said. "His world has key elements to sustain human life—"

"As does Dr. Mann's," Cooper pointed out.

"Cooper," Brand said, shooting him a look, "this is my field. And I really believe Edmunds' planet is the better prospect."

"Why?" he asked.

"Gargantua, that's why," she said. She stepped over to the display. "Look at Miller's world—hydrocarbons, organics, yes. But no life. Sterile. We'll find the same thing on Dr. Mann's."

"Because of the black hole?" Romilly asked.

She nodded. "Murphy's Law—whatever can happen will happen. Accident is the first building block of evolution—but if you're orbiting a black hole not enough *can* happen. It sucks in asteroids and comets, random events that would otherwise reach you. We need to go further afield."

Murphy's Law. In an instant he was back home, leaning on the truck, explaining to Murph that her name wasn't something bad, that it was really an affirmation that life brought surprises, both good and bad. That he and Erin were prepared to deal with things as they came.

He knew he needed to focus on the moment. He understood what Brand was trying to say, and it sounded like a good argument. But he also knew there was something else behind her words, and Edmunds' planet was so much further away...

"You once referred to Dr. Mann as the 'best of us,'" Cooper said. He felt a tickle of conscience—he knew he was setting her up. But this was too important to let it slide.

"He's remarkable," Brand agreed, without hesitation. "We're only here because of him."

"And he's there on the ground, sending us an unambiguous message that we should go to that planet," Cooper said.

Brand's lips thinned, but she didn't say anything.

Romilly looked back and forth between them. He looked a little uncomfortable, perhaps sensing there was something going on beneath the surface of the conversation—something to which he was not privy.

"Should we vote?" Romilly asked.

Cooper didn't feel good about what he was about to do. But now wasn't really the time to worry about anyone's feelings.

"If we're going to vote," he said to Romilly, "there's something you need to know." He paused. "Brand?"

She didn't take the bait, but remained silent.

"He has a right to know," Cooper insisted.

"That has nothing to do with it," she said.

"*What* does?" Romilly asked.

Cooper left her a pause, but when she didn't fill it, he did.

"She's in love with Wolf Edmunds," Cooper told him.

Romilly's brow went up.

"Is that true?" he asked.

Brand looked stricken.

"Yes," she admitted. "And that makes me want to follow my heart. But maybe we've spent too long trying to figure all this with theory—"

"You're a scientist, Brand—" Cooper cut in.

"I am," she said. "So listen to me when I tell you that love isn't something we invented. It's observable, powerful. Why shouldn't it mean something?"

"It means social utility," Cooper said. "Child rearing, social bonding—"

"We love people who've died," Brand objected. "Where's the social utility in that? Maybe it means more— something we can't understand yet. Maybe it's some evidence, some artifact of higher dimensions that we can't consciously perceive. I'm drawn across the universe to someone I haven't seen for a decade, who I know is probably dead. Love is the one thing we're capable of perceiving that transcends dimensions of time and space.

"Maybe we should trust that, even if we can't yet understand it." She sent a pleading look to Romilly, but he couldn't meet her eyes. Cooper could guess what he was thinking—that Brand had probably lost it.

Or at least some of "it."

She saw it, too, and so she brought her appeal back to him.

"Cooper, yes," Brand conceded, wearily. "The tiniest possibility of seeing Wolf again excites me. But that doesn't mean I'm *wrong*."

Cooper had a sudden sense of déjà vu, and remembered his conversation with Donald on the porch.

"I'm not gonna lie to you, Donald," he'd said. *"Heading out there is what I feel born to do, and it excites me. That doesn't make it wrong."*

"Honestly, Amelia," Cooper said gently, "it might."

Brand seemed to wilt. She knew she had lost. He felt for her, but he had to do what made sense. What got this done most quickly and certainly.

"Tars," he said, "set course for Dr. Mann."

Before she turned away, Cooper saw the tears start in Brand's eyes.

After they were out of orbit and on their new trajectory, he found her. She was checking on the population bomb.

"Brand, I'm sorry," he said.

"Why?" she asked, but her voice was tight. "You're just being objective—unless you're punishing me for screwing up on Miller's planet."

"This wasn't a personal decision for me," he said.

She turned from the metal and glass contraption and looked him straight in the eye. He felt her hurt and anger like a heat lamp on his face. It was surprising, in a way, to see her usual detachment so thoroughly compromised.

"Well, if you're wrong, you'll have a *very* personal decision to make," she told him, a good fraction of acid in her tone. "Your fuel calculations are based on a return journey. Strike out on Dr. Mann's planet, and we'll have to decide whether to return home, or push on to Edmunds' planet with plan B. Starting a colony could save us from extinction."

She closed the panel.

"You might have to decide between seeing your children again… and the future of the human race." She smiled, but there was nothing happy or friendly about it.

"I trust you'll be as objective then," she finished.

Murph stood with Tom, watching the field burn. Or, rather, the corn. Because Murph suddenly saw that each plant was its own fire—an incandescent stalk giving itself, spark by spark, to the dark black boil above the light, driving the smoke pointlessly toward the heavens. For a moment she comprehended each of them as filaments in a bulb, flames in a lantern, superheated rods of metal, an alien forest on a distant world. Each plant the maker and center of its own immolation, each burning alone. To say the field was burning was to miss what was really happening. A field was an abstraction. A single plant was not.

It was a life, being sacrificed so that others might survive.

Then the stalks came apart like paper, the updraft shredding some into rising shards, others slumping and crumbling into glowing piles; then that illusion faded, too. Soon there would be no corn, no field. Only carbon and dust, inseparable in their lifelessness.

"We lost about a third this season," Tom said. "But next year… I'm gonna start working Nelson's fields. Should make it up."

Murph wanted to shake him, to make him understand that it would never be "made up." But what was the point?

"What happened to Nelson?" she asked.

The expression on his face suggested she probably didn't want to know, so she didn't press it. This place, its people, the house she had grown up in—it all seemed so remote, and a little unreal to her now.

Tom started for the house, so she followed him. Behind them, the field continued its cremation.

Murph tried to appear interested in her food that evening, as Tom and Lois made small talk about the farm, and their six-year-old, Coop, sent her grins and made faces at her. The little boy reminded her of his namesake, in a lot of ways. Maybe more than he reminded her of Tom.

"Will you stay the night?" Lois asked. "We left your room like it was. My sewing machine's in there, but…"

Murph studied her plate, pushing the food around. She liked Lois well enough, and she was certainly a good partner for Tom—dependable, sturdy, compassionate. Beyond that, Murph didn't know her that well. She kept her visits short, and beyond the subject of farming, they didn't have a lot of common ground.

"No," she said, preparing an excuse. "I need to…"

Her gaze wandered toward the upstairs, then back to Lois, and she knew she didn't want to lie to her.

"Too many memories, Lois," she said.

Lois nodded in understanding.

"We may have something for that," Tom said, as he and

Coop started to take the dishes into the kitchen. As Coop took Murph's plate, he began coughing—an awful, deep-chested cough.

The boy must have seen the concern on her face, because he started grinning at her.

"The dust," he told her. Like it was nothing. As if being sick was just part of it these days, like a stubbed toe or a bloody nose. Normal childhood stuff no one could do a thing about.

Was that how Tom saw things? He might. Otherwise he would have asked her if she could do anything. Even if he didn't really understand what she did, he knew she had access to science and medicine that most folks didn't.

"I have a friend who should have a look at his lungs, Lois," she said, as Tom and Coop went into the kitchen.

Lois nodded, and seemed about to say something when Tom came back in with a bottle of whiskey and sat down. Murph frowned briefly, but didn't say anything.

Outside, she saw clouds of dust, rolling across the twilight plain.

On the drive back, churning across the same battered road she traveled with her father all those years ago, Murph wondered about Lois's reluctance to discuss the idea of Coop seeing a doctor. Was she afraid Tom would see it as some kind of concession—an admission that he couldn't provide everything his son needed? Or worse, would it force him to admit—to himself as much as anyone else—that things were getting worse?

But it wasn't just Coop. It was getting worse for everyone, she knew. More people were getting sick—and staying that way. What had happened to Nelson? It was Tom who didn't want to talk about that.

Projections showed that respiratory ailments were on the rise both in number of the afflicted and the severity, and dust was only part of the problem. Elevated nitrogen levels were taking their toll on human health, as well— directly and indirectly. In the seas, excessive nitrogen was causing widespread algae blooms and huge pockets of hypoxic waters, especially in shallow environments where reefs had once thrived. That, added to the climatic changes that had shifted major currents, was driving the greatest marine extinction since the Permian period—which was to say in the history of the planet.

Once the seas were dead, or mostly so, it would only be a very brief matter of time before what was left of the terrestrial ecosystem crashed. Life itself wasn't in danger— bacteria, for instance, would continue to thrive. But an environment capable of supporting human life? That could be numbered in less than a handful of decades. Maybe. If they were lucky.

Not that most people knew any of this. If you listened to the news, things were just about to turn around. "Any day now." Only she and a relative few others knew the truth. Without plan A, everyone on Earth was going to be dead in a generation. Two, at best.

She had spent all of her adult life dealing with the big end of that, with trying to save the race. But here she was at the other end of things, watching her nephew hack up his lungs. What if Coop, like his brother Jesse, didn't survive long enough for plan A to begin?

She didn't have to let that happen, whatever Tom did or didn't believe. She could do something about it.

Suddenly she was distracted by a noise, and realized that the radio was trying to get her attention.

* ✳ *

Doctor Getty met her as soon as she arrived, and started hustling her down the corridor.

Getty was a pleasantly boyish fellow. She liked his eyes, and his smile was nice, too. He wasn't smiling now, though. His eyes were full of concern—and worse, compassion. They said what he wasn't quite willing to vocalize.

"He started asking for you after he came to," Getty explained apologetically, "but we couldn't raise you…"

When they reached the room, she felt a little faint. Even bound to his wheelchair, there had always been something robust about Professor Brand, an energy that kept him going. You could see it in his eyes, hear it in his voice.

Now, shockingly, she saw that it was gone, or almost so. He seemed tiny in the hospital bed, dwarfed by the machines monitoring him and keeping him alive. When she reached his bedside, she could barely hear his breathing.

"Murph? Murph," he murmured.

She took his hand.

This isn't happening, she thought. *I'm not ready for this.*

"I'm here, Professor," she said.

"I don't have much life…" He gasped for another breath. "I have to tell you…"

"Try to take it easy," Murph said.

"All these… years. All these people… counted on me."

"It's okay, Professor," she reassured him.

"I let… you all… down."

"No," Murph said, close to crying. "I'll finish what you started."

He looked up at her, tears welling over the failing light in his eyes.

"Murph," he said. "Good, good, Murph. I told you to have faith… to believe…"

"I do believe," Murph told him.

"I needed you to believe your father was coming back," he said.

"I do, Professor," she said.

"Forgive me, Murph," he said.

"There's nothing to forgive," she said. But there was such anguish on his face, such abject shame. After all he had done, how could he feel like this? It wasn't fair that he should die feeling as if he was a failure.

"I *lied*, Murph," he sighed.

She blinked, wondering what the hell he could mean. Lied about what?

"I lied to you," he went on. "There's no reason to come back... no way to help us..."

"But plan A," she said, confused. "All this—all these people—the equation!"

He slowly turned his head from side to side, tears streaming down his face. Then he sighed again, and his eyes weren't looking at her anymore. His breath ebbed out slowly, and when it was time to draw another, his chest hardly moved.

"Did he know?" she whispered, desperately. "Did my dad know? Did he abandon me?"

His lips moved as he tried to say something else.

She leaned closer.

"Do... not... go... gentle... into..."

"Into..."

"No!" she shouted. "No! Professor, stay! You can't. You can't leave!"

Getty was suddenly there.

"You can't," she said. "You can't, you..."

Getty put his hand gently on her shoulder, and together they watched the life leave Professor Brand. Her question still floated around her, with no answer coming.

TWENTY-THREE

By the time Murph got up the nerve to send a message to Professor Brand's daughter, her grief and confusion had become something else altogether.

"Dr. Brand," she began, trying to stay in control, to keep her voice even and professional. "I'm sorry to tell you that your father died today. He had no pain and was... at peace." She paused and added, "I'm sorry for your loss."

She reached for the switch, to leave the lie where it lay. Odds were Brand would never hear the message, and if she did—well, she was in space, far from home. She would need comfort, and ..

Murph pulled her hand back.

Amelia was his daughter. His *daughter*, part of the whole thing. She had trusted her father, and he had betrayed her so completely—her father had left her. Who and what was there left for her to trust?

Professor Brand had been a liar. She was not.

At peace, my ass. she thought bitterly. *He died in agony for what he had done.* And if when he stopped breathing he did find some sort of peace, he didn't deserve it.

And he hadn't answered her goddamn question, hadn't

given her the only answer she cared about. No, he had used his last freaking breath to freaking quote Dylan Thomas one last freaking time.

"Did you know, Brand?" she shouted. "Did he tell you? Did you know that plan A was a sham? You knew, didn't you? You left us here. To die.

"Never coming back…"

On the *Endurance*, Case registered Murph's angry message as he watched the Ranger dwindle, carrying the others to the white world beyond the cockpit glass.

TWENTY-FOUR

Cooper studied Mann's world as they approached the cloud cover, which looked for all the world like the fluffy cumulonimbus clouds of Earth—majestic and white, with high, curved peaks and deep, shadowy valleys. That seemed like a good sign, although they were so thick that he couldn't see anything beneath them.

As they drew even nearer, he began to worry. What the heads-up display was telling him about the density of these clouds seemed... unreasonable. Nevertheless, he killed most of their downward velocity, hoping the instruments were wrong, yet unwilling to take chances.

Not after Miller's world.

He banked, cutting through one of the clouds, which to his relief seemed to be entirely normal. Maybe it *was* the instruments that were screwy.

But as they entered the next one, a horrible shudder went through the Ranger. There was a terrible scraping sound as they lost some of the thermo panels on the wing.

Goddammit, he thought. *Why can't anything just be what it seems to be?* Just as the mountains on Miller's world hadn't been mountains, most of these clouds weren't just

clouds. They were formations of frozen carbon dioxide—
dry ice—sublimating to create a deceptively delicate sheath
of vapor around them.

Grateful that he had trusted his gut, and not gone
plowing straight into them, he banked again. He picked
his way gingerly, proceeding as if through a frozen
minefield, taking direction from Tars. And always
following the beacon.

As a kid he'd once flown cross-country on a commercial
airliner. Back then, as they passed through and above a
wonderland of clouds, he had fantasized about being able
to walk on them, ride them across the sky.

It looked like he would get his chance.

Be careful what you wish for, he mused.

They approached the beacon. The signal was coming
from high on a frozen cloud mountain. Cooper gave the
radar profile a quick once-over, and was convinced that
he didn't want to park right next to it. The icy platform it
presented was too small and unstable. Instead, he settled
for a larger, flatter, denser stretch a little below it.

Once down, they began fastening their helmets, but
without the blind rush that had driven them on Miller's
world. They were well beyond Gargantua's time-bending
zone, so there was no point in charging headlong into
things. He took a good long scan around them to make sure
something nasty wasn't coming up from beneath, dropping
down from above, or sneaking in from the sides.

Still, there wasn't a lot of time to waste, so once he felt
pretty secure about the stability of their perch, Tars opened
the hatch. Stepping carefully out of the airlock and onto
the ice, the four of them began hiking up-slope toward
the beacon, Tars bringing up the rear. Cooper hoped

desperately that they weren't in for another game of hide and seek.

But when he crested the ridge he saw it instantly—an orange smudge nestled in the drifts of ice-shatter. He picked up his pace, and soon was gazing at the iced-over form of a Lazarus pod. Tars moved up behind him and began to dig it out, while Cooper prepared for the worst. Mann could easily be as dead as Miller, except this time there would be a body to view. He glanced at Brand and Romilly, and saw the same dread hanging on their expressions.

Once the craft's airlock was clear and open, Cooper stepped in cautiously. The cabin was empty of life, eerie in the faint blue light filtering through the icy windows. Then Tars powered the module up and the lights came on. Cooper saw the cryo-chamber and moved toward it, as Tars clanked along behind him. With his gloved hand he brushed ice from the nameplate.

Dr. Mann, it read.

After a quick status check, Tars activated the cryo-chamber, and the ice began to melt. While he did that, Cooper shut the airlock again. Once it was sealed and the air cycled, he doffed his helmet. The air was stale, but breathable, and tinged with the slight acrid scent of ammonia. There was a mechanical robot, like Tars and Case, lying off to one side, dismantled.

After a short time the cryo-bed signaled all was ready, and Cooper cracked the lid open, revealing the plastic-shrouded figure inside. He was still ready for the worst. The water around the body was now a bit warm, and vapor drifted up into the chilly air.

Cooper found the seal in the plastic, and ripped it open.

A man about his own age lay there. His squared-off face was strong even in sleep, but as Cooper watched, his eyes flickered open, blue, at first without focus, looking at nothing. Then—confused and maybe frightened—he reached for Cooper with trembling hands and grabbed him, embraced him cheek to cheek.

Mann began sobbing, caressing Cooper's face as if it was the face of his mother. Cooper didn't mind, and was in fact overwhelmed by a deep compassion for the man. Unable to even imagine what he was feeling, he just held him tightly, the way he had held his kids when they woke from a nightmare.

"It's okay," he said. "It's okay."

"Pray you never learn just how good it can be, just to see another face."

Mann spoke in a husky voice. His hands shook his mug of tea as he took a sip from it. He looked from face to face, as if each was the most amazing thing he had ever seen.

"I hadn't much hope to begin with," he went on. "After so much time, I had none. My supplies were exhausted. The last time I went to sleep, I set no waking date. You have literally raised me from the dead."

Cooper shot him a smile.

"Lazarus," he said.

Mann nodded, then flicked his eyes up.

"And the others?" he asked.

"I'm afraid you're it, sir," Romilly said.

Mann looked a little stunned.

"So *far*, surely?" Mann said hopefully.

"With our situation," Cooper told him, "there's not much hope of any other rescue."

It was almost as if Cooper had punched him. Mann looked down at his tea, dazed by grief. They let him have his moment of silence.

"Dr. Mann,' Brand said, after a bit, "tell us about your world."

"My world," he said softly. "Yes. Our world, we hope. Our world is cold, stark, but undeniably beautiful…"

"The days are sixty-seven cold hours," Mann told them. "The nights are sixty-seven far colder hours…"

He turned and led them back toward the shelter of his landing craft.

"The gravity is a very pleasant eighty percent of Earth's," he said. "Up here, where I landed, the 'water' is alkali and the 'air' has too much ammonia in it to breathe for more than a few minutes. But down on the surface—and there is a surface—the ammonia gives way to crystalline hydrocarbons and breathable air. To organics. Possibly even to life. Yes, we may be sharing this world."

Brand began checking Mann's data, and the more she read, the more she seemed positively giddy. Finally she looked up from the screen.

"These readings are from the surface?" she asked, as if it didn't seem real.

"Over the years I've dropped various probes," Mann confirmed.

"How far have you explored?" Cooper asked.

"I've mounted several major expeditions," Mann said. "But with oxygen in limited supply, Kipp there had to do most of the legwork." He indicated the machine that could have been a brother to Tars or Case, except that it was lying about in various pieces.

"What's wrong with him?" Tars asked.

"Degeneration," Mann replied. "He misidentified the first organics we found as ammonia crystals. We struggled on for a time, but ultimately I decommissioned him and used his power source to keep the mission going." He shook his head sadly. "I thought I was alone *before* I shut him down."

"Would you like me to look at him?" Tars asked.

"No," Mann said. "He needs a human touch."

Tars didn't reply. Instead he turned abruptly to Brand.

"Dr. Brand," he said, "Case is relaying a message for you from the comm station."

She nodded, and Tars began the playback on his data screen.

Cooper's stomach clenched as the face of a woman appeared. It took a moment for him to recognize it as the face of his daughter.

Murph!

But she wasn't calling *him*, she was calling Brand, and worse, Murph was delivering the news that Brand's father was dead. He couldn't tell which of the two women seemed more upset at the news, but it looked as if it was Murph.

"He had no pain and was… at peace," she was saying. "I'm sorry for your loss."

"Is that Murph?" Brand asked in an abstract voice.

Cooper nodded and tried to think of something to say as he watched Murph reach to turn the camera off.

"She's become a—" Brand began, but she didn't finish, because Murph didn't turn off the camera. She pulled her hand back, and a strange look came over her. Anger, instant and intense.

"Did you know, Brand?" Murph demanded furiously. "Did he tell you? That plan A was a sham? You knew, didn't you? You left us here. To die.

"Never coming back…"

Stunned, Cooper stared at Brand's face, watched the shock run across it. He wanted to ask what the *hell* she was talking about, but couldn't find the words.

"You left us here to set up your colony," Murph went

on, tears starting down her cheeks. He stared aghast as she struggled with her next words, and he knew. He knew what she was going to ask.

As quickly as it had appeared, the anger was gone, and her voice became very small.

"Did my father know?" she asked. "Dad…?"

And somehow, over impossible distance and through strange, twisted time, she was looking straight into his eyes.

"Did you leave me here to die?"

Then the screen did go dark, and he felt the whole of himself ache and he knew it was true, that he should have known. Should *always* have known.

Suddenly he realized that Brand was staring at him.

"Cooper," she said, "my father devoted his whole life to plan A. I have no idea what she means—"

"I do," Mann said quietly. Cooper turned to find him looking at them with an expression of gentle compassion. But before he could continue, Cooper found his voice.

"He never even hoped to get people off Earth," he said. He felt husked out, like a stalk of corn rotted by the blight. Empty for the moment, although he was certain the pain would come.

"No," Mann confirmed.

"But he's been trying to solve the gravity equation for forty years!" Brand protested.

Mann stepped closer and regarded her empathetically.

"Amelia," he said, "your father solved his equation before I even left."

"Then why wouldn't he use it?" she asked, in a tortured voice.

"The equation couldn't reconcile relativity with quantum mechanics," he told her. "You need more."

"More what?" Cooper demanded.

"More data," he replied. "You need to see inside a black

hole. And the laws of nature prohibit a naked singularity."

"Is that true?" Cooper asked Romilly. The astrophysicist nodded.

"If a black hole is an oyster," Romilly explained, "the singularity is the pearl inside. Its gravity is so strong, it's always hidden in darkness, behind the horizon. That's why we call it a black hole."

"If we could look beyond the horizon—" Cooper said.

"Some things aren't meant to be known," Mann told him.

That's it? Cooper wondered. *That's all you've got?* It seemed to him an absurd thing for a scientist to say. Like the fox in the fable, unable to reach the grapes, declaring they must be sour anyhow. But how many times in history had that declaration been made, and how often had those who said it been proven wrong?

The black hole was right there.

There had to be a way.

Mann turned to speak to Brand again.

"Your father had to find another way to save the human race from extinction," he said. "Plan B. A colony."

Yet Brand still wasn't willing to give up the point. That made Cooper feel better, because he didn't think she was acting. She hadn't been in on it. Hadn't been lying to him all of this time.

"But why not tell people?" Brand demanded. "Why keep building the damn station?"

"How much harder would it be for people to come together and save the species instead of themselves?" Mann gave Cooper a sympathetic glance. "Or their children?"

"Bullshit," Cooper said flatly.

"Would *you* have left, if you hadn't believed you were trying to save *them*?" Mann challenged. "Evolution has yet to transcend that simple barrier—we can care deeply, selflessly for people we know, but our empathy rarely extends beyond our line of sight."

"But the lie," Brand said, her voice low and disbelieving. "The monstrous lie…"

"Unforgivable," Mann agreed. "And he knew it. Your father was prepared to destroy his own humanity to save our species. He made the ultimate sacrifice."

"No," Cooper said, feeling the boil, the fury at so ludicrous a claim: that the sacrifice of one man's reputation rose anywhere near the level of "ultimate."

"No," he said grimly. "That's being made by the people of Earth, who'll die because in his arrogance, he declared *their* case hopeless."

Mann gave him a look, and under other circumstances his expression might have seemed earnest. Now it only seemed condescending.

"I'm sorry, Cooper," he said. "Their case *is* hopeless. We are the future."

Then the bottom dropped out of everything. Cooper realized that he should have known better. He had just been so damned eager to get back into space, he'd been prepared to believe any goddamn thing Professor Brand said.

"*I'm asking you to trust me,*" he'd said. "*When you return, I'll have solved the problem of gravity. You have my word.*"

Brand put a hand on his shoulder, but he didn't move.

"Cooper," she said. "What can I do?"

He took a moment.

"Let me go home," he said.

PART THREE

TWENTY-FIVE

A muddy dawn filtered through the dusty sky as Murph steered the pickup. Smoke rose in black pillars from burning fields, like offerings to some savage god of old.

"Are you sure?" Dr. Getty asked from the passenger's seat.

"The solution was correct," she said. "He'd had it for years."

"It's worthless?"

"It's *half* the answer," she said. She saw more dust ahead, probably kicked up by traffic on the road.

"How do you find the other half?" he asked.

She released one hand from the wheel and pointed to the sky.

"Out there?" she said. "A black hole. Stuck here on Earth? I'm not sure you can."

They were near enough to see the convoy now, trucks and cars piled high with clothes, furniture—whole households of belongings reduced to what a car could hold. Their owners were packed in wherever they could find space.

"They just pack up and leave," Getty observed in a puzzled tone. "What are they hoping to find?"

"Survival," she said. Then she saw it—the wall of

dust, the black blizzard bearing down on them like an unstoppable juggernaut.

"Dammit!" she said as it rushed over them, eclipsing the road, the empty storefronts and abandoned houses, erasing everything from their sight. Inside of the cloud, it might as well have been night.

She pulled over and turned the engine off. They sat there, the truck rocking in the wind as the dust began trying to bury them in earnest. She remembered another storm—the last one she had been in with her family, before the coordinates appeared on her bedroom floor. She remembered her father's concentration, his determination to get them home safe.

Murph remembered, too, the validation she had felt after they reached the house, when he saw the pattern, and took it seriously. It had felt like such a victory.

And yet he had never taken the rest of it seriously.

Her ghost.

The books.

How could he have been so selective? she wondered. *Why hadn't he wanted to know what it all meant, rather than focusing on the easy part?* But she knew the answer— most likely she always had. He'd only been interested in the part that told him what he wanted to hear: that he had been chosen, that it was his *destiny* to go into space. He'd kept his focus narrow on purpose, so things would remain simple, and his decision would be easy because it was inevitable.

She wondered, now, if she hadn't been doing the same thing for years. Was there something she was missing— some bigger picture that had been obscured by her anger? By the hurt of him leaving? Had she trusted the professor so much because she needed to feel she had someone trustworthy in her life? She should have seen what he was up to—or rather, wasn't up to—years ago. Instead she had blindly bumped her head against his self-imposed barrier for decades. Narrow focus. Keep it simple.

Just like Dad.

It was like the problem with gravity—trying to make the theory of relativity mesh with quantum theory. Both worked fine in describing the nature of the universe, each on a different scale—the very large in the case of relativity, and the very small in quantum theory. But held side by side they seemed contradictory. In the singularity inside a black hole, the two must come together and be merged.

Yet the universe *was*. It existed, and it worked. Somehow. So the apparent contradiction wasn't in the physical world—it was the result of imperfect data, a wrong way of looking at things. Faulty equations based on mistaken assumptions.

Her ghost wrote with gravity, pushed books from their shelves with it. Her ghost told her father where to go, how to leave—and then it begged him to stay. Could that contradiction be reconciled, or was one end or the other of that equation just plain wrong?

She had been ten. Maybe the Morse code interpretation had been wishful thinking—an attempt to interpret data the way she *wanted* it to be interpreted. The floor pattern, after all, had been binary.

And yet Morse was binary, in a way…

"Don't people have the right to know?" Getty asked, cutting off her ruminations.

She'd thought about that, pondered the lie. But she had also begun to come to terms with it, in a way. Not with the professor himself, but with the illusion he had maintained.

"Panic won't help," she said. "We have to keep working, same as ever."

"Isn't that just what Professor Brand—?"

"Brand gave up on us," she snapped, her anger flaring.

"I'm still trying to solve this."

"So you have an idea?" Getty asked.

"No," she said. "I have a feeling."

She felt his gaze on her as she stared out into the dust.

"I told you about my ghost," she said, after a few heartbeats.

She remembered being ten, just out of the shower, her hair wet, a towel around her neck, finding the book on the floor and the broken lunar lander model beside it.

She placed her hand on the car window, watching the dust sleet by, looking for patterns in it. Equations. Morse code. *"Murph, you wanna talk science, don't just tell me you're scared of some ghost. Record the facts, analyze— present your conclusions."*

"My dad thought I called it a ghost because I was scared of it," she told Getty. "But I was never scared of it." She remembered counting the books, drawing lines to represent them. Trying to decode the message—because she *knew* there was a message.

She turned from the window and regarded Dr. Getty once again. Why was she telling him this? She had mentioned the ghost to him once, but she had left it at that—the story of a childhood mystery. And yet she had never told anyone else even *that* much. And now she was babbling on…

Maybe it was because he wasn't a mathematician or an astrophysicist, because the concerns of their work didn't overlap much. He wouldn't know when she was stepping from the terrain of the accepted into the *terra incognita* of La-la Land. Or maybe he was just a good listener. Or it could be because he was here, now, in her little bubble in the dust, and she felt for some reason that there was an urgency about all of this.

"I called it that because it felt like—like a person," she

went on. "Trying to tell me something…"

The dust was thinning as the wind dropped off.

A short one this time, thank God.

She started the engine.

"If there's an answer here on Earth," she said, "it's back there, somehow. No one's coming to save us."

She pulled back onto the road, such as it was, and continued on.

"I have to find it," she said.

She pulled past a pickup, stuffed almost comically with belongings and passengers. But there was nothing comical about the two kids in back, the dust smeared on their faces and clothes, the lost look in their eyes.

"We're running out of time," she said.

TWENTY-SIX

Cooper propped his feet up on the console of the Ranger, and watched through the windshield as Case brought the lander down, its braking rockets flaring before it gently settled onto the ice. The lander wasn't as sleek as the Rangers—it was a bit boxier, more plough horse than racehorse, handsome rather than beautiful.

Tars was out on the wing of the Ranger, making repairs.

"What about auxiliary oxygen scrubbers?" Case asked via radio.

"They can stay," Cooper said. "I'll sleep most of the journey." He smiled sardonically. "I saw it all on the way out here."

In his mind, he was already on the way home, but in fact, there was a great deal to do before he could get off. Anything he could live without—like the auxiliary scrubbers—would be left behind, for Brand, Romilly, and Mann to use in building humanity's "future."

Likewise, there was a lot of stuff that needed to be brought down from the *Endurance*—obvious things like the population bomb with its cargo of unborn, but also anything else they might possibly need. It would be an ongoing process—the *Endurance* had made her last voyage, and while fuel remained the crew would continue to cannibalize the ring-ship for parts, until they became capable of finding, extracting, and processing the natural resources of their new home.

It was only fair that he help them begin the process. After all the time he'd lost, another day or two wouldn't make much difference.

He looked up as Romilly came through the airlock and released his helmet. It still came as a bit of a shock, seeing the age on him. And it served as a reminder of what he faced if he managed to return to Earth.

"I have a suggestion for your return journey," Romilly said.

"What?" Cooper asked.

"Have one last crack at the black hole."

Behind Romilly, Tars entered the ship.

"Gargantua's an older, spinning black hole," Romilly went on. "What we call a gentle singularity."

"Gentle?" He remembered the force yanking them toward Miller's world, the nearly two-mile-high tidal waves, the razor's edge of naught that was Gargantua's horizon.

"They're hardly gentle," Romilly qualified, "but their tidal gravity is quick enough that something crossing the horizon fast enough might survive… a probe, say."

"What happens to it after it crosses?" Cooper asked.

"Beyond the event horizon is a complete mystery," Romilly said. "Who's to say there isn't some way the probe can glimpse the singularity and relay the quantum data? If he's equipped to transmit every form of energy that can pulse—X-ray, visible light, radio…"

"Just when did this probe become a 'he?'" Cooper asked.

Romilly suddenly looked awkward.

"Tars is the obvious candidate," he said, sheepishly.

"I've already told him what to look for."

"I'd need to take the old optical telescope from Kipp," Tars said in his matter-of-fact way.

Cooper regarded Tars. If there was still any chance for plan A, didn't they have to take it? But at what cost? Sure, Tars was a machine, but he was a person, too—in a way.

"You'd do this for us?" Cooper asked the machine.

"Before you get teary," Tars said, "try to remember that as a robot I have to do anything you say, anyway."

"Your cue light's broken," Cooper said, when no LED came on.

"I'm not joking," Tars replied.

Only then did the light flash on.

Brand and Mann met him at the foot of the ladder.

"Ranger's almost ready," Cooper told them. "Case is on his way back with another load."

"I'll start a final inventory," Brand offered.

"Dr. Mann," Romilly said, "I need Tars to remove and adapt some components from Kipp."

Mann cocked his head and regarded the robot for a moment.

"He mustn't disturb Kipp's archival functions."

"I'll supervise," Romilly assured him.

Mann still seemed reluctant, but then he nodded.

Cooper listened to the exchange a little impatiently. He had his own concerns. He didn't feel as if he could leave until a couple of things had been dealt with. First and foremost they needed to establish the location of the colony Brand, Mann and the rest would found. He could bring that information back to Earth, in case they *did* manage to send another expedition. And it would also ease his mind to see the place, to know concretely that his friends—that the human race — had a new home.

"We need to pick out a site," Cooper told Mann. "You don't wanna have to move the module once we land it."

"I'll show you the probe sites," Mann said, as a hard wind blustered across the frozen cloudscape.

"Will conditions hold?" Cooper asked, eyeing the sky.

"These squalls usually blow over," Mann said. "You've got a long-range transmitter?"

Cooper checked the box plugged into the neck-ring of his spacesuit.

"Good to go," he said.

Mann pointed at the thrust nozzle in his elbow joint.

"Charged?" he asked. Cooper double-checked and gave him a thumbs up.

Without further hesitation, they set off. After a few moments, the lander passed over them, with Case at the controls. Cooper reached up and keyed his long-range transmitter.

"A little caution, Case?" he said.

"Safety first, Cooper," Case shot back.

Cooper and Mann tracked on over the sculpted ice, the surface grinding beneath their boots.

Cooper had changed his mind about Mann's world as he got to know it better. It was nothing like any place on Earth. Where they now walked, the clouds were no longer white, but rather a sort of charcoal color, as if they were frozen thunderheads. Of course, he knew that the color came from minerals frozen in the ice, and there were probably places on Earth with similar dirty snow. But nowhere on his home planet did any glacier rise into such strange configurations, spreading in the sky above, dropping off into blue darkness below, winding into formations like gigantic, frozen worms.

After a time they came to an edge, and a drop of about fifty feet.

"Just take it gently," Mann said, stepping off the cliff. The jets at his elbows flared, slowing him so he landed with a light thump instead of a splat. A little less sure of himself, Cooper followed.

The lighter gravity made everything seem a little dreamlike, even in the heavy suit. Acceleration didn't feel quite right, nor did the kick of his thrusters when he fired them. Evolution had built his brain for thirty-two feet per second per second, and that wasn't how physics played here.

He landed in a massive canyon of ice. Beautiful, as Mann had said, but also daunting. It made him feel insignificant. Gazing at the wind-sculpted walls, he wondered how old the ice was, what forces other than wind had shaped it. What the unseen surface below was like. Mann said there was air present, and organics, but with this superstrata of frozen clouds it was going to be dark, wasn't it? And cold, probably much colder than up above.

He imagined the plan B kids, born into that dark, icy world. Romilly and Brand would tell tales of a warmer, sunnier place, but in a few generations those stories would be forgotten, and permanent night and winter would be all they would know

Was this what "they" had planned? Their mysterious benefactors who scribbled coordinates with gravity?

Somehow it didn't seem like enough.

Maybe he was wrong. Maybe it wasn't dark down there — maybe the ice splintered the light into constant rainbows, and geothermal forces created hot spots as comfortable as any tropical paradise. Mann seemed confident enough in the place.

Anyway, it was almost out of his hands now. He was nearly quit of plan B.

Then he realized Mann was talking to him.

"Brand told me why you feel you have to go back," he said.

Cooper set his feet. He'd been afraid of this.

"If this little excursion is about trying to change my mind," he said, "let's turn around right now."

"No," Mann assured him. "I understand your position."

He turned and continued walking.

Still a little suspicious, Cooper followed.

"You have attachments," Mann went on. "I'm not supposed to, but even without family, I can promise you that the yearning to be with other people is massively powerful. Our instincts, our emotions, are at the foundations of what makes us human. They're not to be taken lightly."

A wind whipped down the canyon, gusting ice crystals between them.

After introducing Getty to Lois and Coop, Murph slipped upstairs to her old bedroom. Part of her was almost afraid of what she might see there, of the memories it would stir. She knew, though... she *knew* that this was where it started, that there was something this place could tell her.

Had been waiting to tell her.

After a little pause, she opened the door.

"Mama lets me play in here."

She realized with a start that Coop had followed her. The boy pointed to a box on one of the shelves.

"I didn't touch your stuff," he said, with the over-earnestness of a child who wasn't telling the truth.

It didn't matter, of course. She didn't have any use for whatever was there, did she? If she had, she would have taken it long ago.

* ✳ *

As Amelia watched the lander descend, she felt a sense of finality come over her, a door closing forever, or like—what was the old expression? As if she was burning the bridge behind her. This was really it. She was going to spend the rest of her life here, watching over plan B, rearing children who would never know any other mother than her, no fathers other than Mann or Romilly.

Cooper was going—and with him all hope for Wolf.

Why didn't you tell me, Dad? she asked the mute ghost of her father. *Why didn't you trust even me?* But what would she have done with that knowledge? Would she have warned Cooper away? Without him, they would never have gotten this far. Would she have been able to lie to him, in the name of the greater good?

Maybe.

Probably. But her father had robbed—or spared—her knowing for sure if she was capable of his sin.

She turned away from the spray of ice as the lander touched down. It didn't matter, did it? There was a lot to be done, and not a lot of time to do it in. But after that—well, there would be more than enough time. And at least she wouldn't be alone. She wasn't sure she would have the strength to do this alone.

Romilly watched as Tars connected the inert Kipp to his own power, thinking about the moment when the robot would cross Gargantua's singularity.

He realized he was jealous of Cooper—not because he was going home but because he would be there when the quantum data started coming in to see it first—if anything did, in fact, come through. The odds were low, but even the smallest chance made it worthwhile. A chance to revive plan A, sure, but also just to *know*, to see whatever it was that could reconcile relativity and quantum mechanics, the very big and the very small... how fantastic that would be! Worth all of it, at least to him, after those long years of staring at Gargantua alone.

Knowing the secret was there.

Knowing he could never see it.

Kipp stirred, and Romilly tried to return his attention to the task in front of him.

Even though he knew better, even though he was aware his suit was keeping him at a comfortable temperature, Cooper felt colder as the wind rose into fitful gales, streaming the ice-dust to hiss against their suits and scour the canyon walls. He began to doubt Mann's prediction that the wind would soon subside.

The doctor was setting a pace that was hard to keep up with, and Cooper found he had dropped back a bit. Mann noticed, and stopped to let him catch up.

"You know why we couldn't just send machines on these missions, Cooper?" Mann asked.

"Frankly, no," Cooper panted. He had been wondering that for a while now. Tars or Case could easily have accomplished what Mann, Miller, and the others had done. Maybe more reliably—Tars might have survived the wave that killed Miller, at least long enough to post a sign on the cosmic bulletin board that said "Keep the hell away from here!"

He caught up, and Mann continued forward.

"A trip into the unknown requires improvisation," he said. "Machines can't improvise well because you can't program a fear of death. The survival instinct is our greatest single source of inspiration."

He stopped and turned to Cooper, a fish-eye view of the

canyon faintly reflected on the glass of his helmet.

"Take you," he said. "A father. With a survival instinct that extends to your kids—"

"That's why I'm going home," Cooper said. "Hopeless or not."

"And what does research tell us is the last thing you'll see before you die?" Mann pushed on.

He acted as if Cooper should know the answer to that, but he didn't have any idea what the scientist was getting at.

What *was* clear was that the conversation was taking a distinctly morbid turn. He couldn't blame Mann for having things to get off his chest after what he'd been through—but couldn't it wait until they were back, comfortable in the lander?

Apparently not, because when he saw that Cooper had no reply, Mann continued.

"Your children," he said, pausing again. "At the very moment of death your mind pushes you a little harder to survive. For them."

Then he started walking again.

Okay, Cooper thought. Maybe Mann had been alone a little *too* long.

When Murph brought Coop back down the stairs, she found Getty with his stethoscope, listening to Lois's back, a grim expression on his face. He shook his head and looked up at her.

"They can't stay here," he said. Before he could continue, however, another voice cut in.

"Murph?"

It was Tom. He was standing in the doorway, looking confused.

"What is this?" her brother asked.

TWENTY-SEVEN

As Kipp came partly to life, data began fluorescing across his screen. Romilly followed it—at first casually, but then with mounting confusion.

He took his helmet off for a better view.

"I don't understand," he murmured.

The canyon lay behind them, and Cooper followed Mann down to a vast plain of ice. He felt dwarfed by it, like a flea on a bed sheet. Wind had striated the ice, carved it into a low relief, almost as if someone had scratched it with their nails.

Lots of someones, actually.

His imagination suddenly summoned an army of thousands of ghostly, ice-colored creatures, defeated in some ancient battle, being dragged off by the victors, their claw-like nails digging futilely into the surface, leaving the marks that remained until the present day...

Back on Earth, he mused, a lot of people used to explain geographic features with such stories—like Paul Bunyan digging the Grand Canyon with his axe. Would it be the same here? Would the kids of plan B call this the "Ghost Scratch Plateau," or something like that?

Probably. A human landscape was a named one. But would they really retreat to the supernatural, or would science stay with them? Would they wonder, as he did, if it ever rained? How the ice was replaced, once the wind blasted it away? Or was it replaced? Maybe all of this had been formed by some sort of massive upheaval, untold years ago, and was inexorably weathering away...

Brand had said that there would be no such geologic events here on Mann's world, due to Gargantua, but maybe she was wrong about that. There might not be any asteroid impacts, yet surely there was—or had been—volcanism. Maybe more than usual, what with a dead star constantly tugging at the planet's crust.

Most of all, he wondered why he was even thinking about it at all. It wasn't as if he was planning to stay.

"The first window's up ahead—" Mann said.

Thank God, Cooper thought. *Let's get this over with.* Ahead, he saw what Mann was talking about—an opening in the ice. The scientist stepped over to the edge.

"When I left Earth, I felt fully prepared to die," Mann told him. "But I just never faced the possibility that my planet wouldn't be the one." His tone turned regretful. "None of this turned out the way it was supposed to."

"Professor Brand would disagree," Cooper said. He peered warily into the depths of the crevasse.

Then he saw movement on the verge of his vision. At first he thought it was Mann going to pat him on the shoulder or something, another of many sympathetic gestures.

Before he could react, however, the scientist ripped Cooper's long-range transmitter from his collar and tossed it away. He was just turning to ask Mann what the hell he thought he was playing at, this close to a freaking *cliff*, when Mann lifted his elbow…

…and blasted him with his thruster. The expanding jet of gas sent Cooper off-balance and he slid back. He just managed not to go over the edge.

"What are you doing?" he demanded, still somehow refusing to accept what was actually happening. It was a prank of some kind, surely… But then Mann kicked at him, and his sense of reality snapped back into place.

The scientist was trying to kill him.

Cooper fired his own thrusters to avoid the attack, which sent him plummeting back over the cliff.

Fortunately it wasn't a sheer drop, but a series of descending shelves, so he landed on the next one down.

Murph watched in horror as Tom placed himself squarely in front of Getty. Her brother's face was growing redder by the moment.

"They can't stay here, Tom," Murph said.

"Not one more day—" Getty began to add, until Tom's fist punctuated his sentence.

Getty dropped like a sack.

"Tom!" Lois gasped.

Tom turned his angry gaze on Murph.

"Coop," he said, "get your aunt's things—she's done here."

"Tom," she pleaded. "Dad didn't raise you this dumb—"

Then Tom exploded.

"Dad didn't raise us!" he bellowed. "Grandpa did, and he's buried outside with Mom, in the ground. I'm *not* leaving them."

"You have to, Tom," she said.

"I'm a farmer, Murph," he replied. "You don't give up on the earth."

"No," she shouted back, "but she gave up on you! And she's poisoning your family!"

By the time Cooper pushed himself up to his knees, Mann was almost on top of him.

"I'm sorry," Mann said. "I can't let you leave."

"Why?" Cooper asked, desperately.

"We're going to need your ship to continue the mission," Mann said, "once the others realize what this place *isn't*."

And it clicked—all of his uneasiness about this place, Mann's strange remarks, the too-perfect news about a surface no one had seen.

"You faked all that data?" Cooper asked, incredulous.

"I had a lot of time," Mann said.

"Is there even a surface?" Cooper asked.

"I'm afraid not."

Cooper saw the kick coming, but there was nothing he could do about it. It knocked him back and down, but he managed to cling to the edge of the ice shelf.

"I tried to do my duty, Cooper," Mann said, "but the day I arrived I could see this place had nothing. I resisted the temptation for years—but I knew there was a way to get rescued."

"You *coward*," Cooper snarled. He jerked up his elbow and fired the thruster at Mann. Unprepared, the scientist went sprawling as Cooper scrambled back up onto the shelf. He managed to find his footing before Mann came back, tackling him, and they both went to the ice, clutching and grasping at each other, wrestling on the edge of the abyss.

* * *

"Please come with us," Murph begged her brother as Getty slowly got to his feet, blood trickling from his nose. She had never seen Tom so angry, so irrational. Somehow, she had to calm him down, make him listen to reason.

"To live underground, praying Dad comes back to save us all?" Tom sneered.

"He's not coming back," Murph said. "He was never coming back. It's up to us. To me."

That was a mistake—she saw it right away.

She wondered, suddenly, if he'd resented her being taken off, educated, treated differently. Being part of their father's world. Fragments of memory came to her. He'd made comments, now and then—his usual sarcastic remarks—but nothing that had added up to this.

"You're gonna save the human race, Murph?" Tom rejoined. "Really? How? Our dad couldn't—"

"He didn't even try!" she shouted. Then, quieter. "He just abandoned us, Tom." But she could see Tom's intractability in the set of his mouth.

Coop handed her the box of her things. He looked so young and earnest, confused.

And sick.

"Tom," she implored him. "If you won't come, let them—"

Tom pointed at the box.

"Take your stuff and go," he said.

She studied it for a moment, the container of things from another life. Then she handed it back to Coop.

"Keep it," she said. Then she left. Getty came with her, silently nursing his jaw.

Mann lunged at him like a madman, but this time Cooper managed to sidestep and grapple him, throwing him to the ground and pinning him there.

"Stop this!" Cooper shouted, his face mere inches from the scientist's. Mann's response was to slam his faceplate into Cooper's, hard, snapping his head back.

Then again.

And again.

"Someone's—glass—will—give—way—first!" he grunted between strikes.

"Fifty-fifty you kill yourself," Cooper howled. "Stop!"

And suddenly Mann did stop. He looked at Cooper with an unreadable expression. His faceplate was already riddled with tiny fractures.

So was Cooper's.

"Best odds I've had in years," Mann told him, and then he butted his head into Cooper's glass. Cooper heard it crack, felt the cold first, and then the acrid, nose-scorching scent of ammonia.

Horrified, he rolled away, trying to cover the crack with his glove, only then realizing how big it was.

As he lay there, he was vaguely aware that Mann was bending over him. He felt the burn in his throat now, and his windpipe tried to close, to keep the poisonous atmosphere out of his lungs.

"Please don't judge me, Cooper," Mann said. "You were never tested like I was. Few men have been..."

Murph's throat was tight as she drove away from the farmhouse and back toward NASA.

"You did your best, Murph," Getty said. He sounded as if he meant it, and she was amazed he could summon that much empathy while nursing his own bleeding nose.

But it wasn't how she felt. She *hadn't* done her best. She'd been glad to be quit of the farm and corn and all of it—as glad as Dad had ever been—to just leave Grandpa and Tom to deal with it. And the result was a chasm between her and her brother, a chasm miles wide and deep and completely invisible to her, until now. Tom was the guy who stayed and did what everyone told him he was supposed to do, working hard at the soil, watching his crops die, watching his children die.

She had followed their absentee father off to save the world in an air-conditioned cave. She had abandoned Tom, too.

Small wonder if he resented her.

But it was Lois and little Coop that would pay the price for what she had done. It was a price they should not have been forced to pay.

TWENTY-EIGHT

Cooper crawled, half blind, across the ice. His face was numb, but his lungs felt like they were on fire. He knew if it wasn't for the positive pressure from his oxygen supply, he would probably already be unconscious. As it was, the toxic air of Mann's world was at least slightly diluted.

That wouldn't help him for long, though. The first black wave of panic was over, replaced by...

"You're feeling it, aren't you?" Mann said. "That survival instinct—that's what drove me. It's always driven the human race, and it's going to save it now. *I'm* going to save it. For all mankind. For you, Cooper."

Mann got up and began walking away.

"I'm sorry," he said over his shoulder. "I can't watch you go through this—I thought I could. But I'm still here. I'm here for you."

"*I'm here for you.*" It was the most terrifying thing Mann had said. *He's really doing this*, Cooper thought. *Mann is really going to let me die. And he thinks he's being nice about it.*

"Cooper," Mann continued, "when you left, did Professor Brand read you the poem? How does it end?"

Cooper saw him climb back up onto the shelf, and knew he would never have the strength to do the same thing. Even if he did...

"Do not go gentle into that good night," Mann said.

Cooper remembered of course—the professor's comforting voice, wishing them farewell as they slipped the shackles of Earth and headed out toward Saturn, the wormhole, the stars beyond. His words had been a guide, a path to follow, a message of hope.

On Mann's lips they were a eulogy.

More bullshit to make him feel clean about murder.

People had always called Cooper stubborn, but he had always thought of himself more as realistic, and perhaps a bit—persistent. Just now he felt something harden in him and compress, like coal being squeezed into a diamond.

He knew, intellectually, that he was going to die someday. He wasn't exactly okay with it, but facts were facts. One day, he would, in fact, go into that "good night." But not today, quietly or any other way. And not by Mann's hands.

No way.

Wasn't going to happen.

His mind boiled away everything but what he needed to know, what he needed to see—and then he saw it, just a few feet away.

The long-range transmitter.

Summoning everything he had, he began crawling toward it, even as black spots began to dance before his eyes and his chest felt as if it were going to explode.

Rage, rage against the dying of the light.

Mann looked back down at Cooper, his tortured coughing and choking as clear in his ears as if he were right there. He had wondered if he would feel regret. He supposed it was still too early to tell. Cooper was still trying, still struggling, still somehow hoping to survive. It was the most magnificent thing he had ever witnessed. He wished the pilot could somehow understand why it was necessary.

He turned away and used his jets to return to the higher ground, and then looked back once more at the feebly thrashing figure.

"Cooper," he said. "Do you see your children yet?"

The only answer was more hacking, and it was all suddenly too much for Mann. It must be so lonely to die, even when someone was with you.

A wave of unanticipated terror swept through him, and he turned off the radio, unable to even listen anymore. Cooper was still moving, a small figure, but at least now he was silent.

Mann put his back to it, and went to do what he must.

Cooper grasped the transmitter, but his gloves might as well have been mittens as he struggled to reconnect it. He tried to slow down, to get it right, but everything was fading, and if he didn't do it soon, it wouldn't get done at all.

But he couldn't do it. Not with the gloves on.

So he pulled them off. He felt the cold again—it struck through his hands and up his arms, encircling his heart, but he could *feel*; for a few seconds the sensation was energizing. But then everything was shaking, and his fingers wouldn't stay still...

Then the transmitter clicked into place.

"Brand!" he rasped out. "Brand! Help me! Help..."

And elsewhere, on a dusty plain, Murph knew what she had to do. She wheeled the truck around and floored it.

* ❄ *

Brand leapt into the cockpit, Cooper's fading voice still ringing in her ears. What had happened? Cooper sounded like he was asphyxiating, and she hadn't heard anything at all from Mann. Was the scientist dead already?

"I have a fix," Case said, as the engines cut in.

"Cooper?" she said. "Cooper, we're coming."

"No air," he wheezed. "Ammonia."

"Don't talk," she said. Breathe as little as possible— we're coming."

Murph pulled off the road and blew into one of Tom's cornfields, cutting through it as Getty sat wide-eyed and white-knuckled in the passenger seat. As she watched the corn part around the bumper, she remembered that long-ago day when they had chased the Indian drone, the three of them—Dad, Tom, and her.

The last time they had done anything together. Tom driving, her keeping the antenna fixed, Dad cracking the encryption. They'd been a team, a family.

Only a day later, all of that had been blown to hell. And now, Tom thought she was the enemy.

Well—she was about to be.

Brand tried to keep steady as Case wove somewhat more than recklessly through the ice formations, avoiding collision sometimes by no more than inches.

It was the same sick feeling in her belly as the one she'd felt when she saw the wave bearing down on them on Miller's world—the realization that not only was everything they knew not enough, but sometimes it actively hurt them.

All of her instincts had told her that a few inches of water was harmless, and that big fluffy clouds were nothing to worry about.

Every assumption they made here was a disaster in the making.

She didn't know how Mann's world had deceived them this time, but she hoped desperately that Case knew what he was doing, where he was going, because Cooper couldn't have much time left.

In Mann's poc, Romilly was still trying to comprehend what he was seeing, and not really getting anywhere. He felt a renewed sense of the frustration he'd felt on the *Endurance*; years alone with the data, talking to himself, on the verge of going crazy—and occasionally maybe veering over that verge.

He remembered what Mann had said about leaving Kipp's archives intact, the tacit implication being that he didn't need to bother with them at all. But this... this was intolerable. Why would Mann warn him off, anyway? Had he stored personal data? Had Kipp witnessed and recorded him acting a little crazy? Romilly could understand that. He'd been there himself. But the fact was, there were some fundamental contradictions here that only a scan of the archives could clear up.

Mann would probably never know, and if he did—well, it was far easier to get forgiveness than permission.

"This data makes no sense," he said to Tars. "Access the archive."

This is good enough, Murph figured.

She hopped out of the truck, lifted the gas can

from the back, and started dousing the cornstalks. She remembered wandering in the fields when she was little, being thoroughly enveloped by them, like being in her own secret maze. She had liked corn, then—the grassy smell of the leaves, the yellow pollen when it tasseled, the ears that appeared almost magically beneath those tufts, swelling daily. The sweet taste of it when it was green, in the milk, before it began to harden into grain.

That had been a real luxury, green corn—a waste of the corn's full potential to feed humanity's masses, but an awesome treat for a kid. To her, it would always be the taste of summer, and of her youth. The idea of burning the corn seemed wrong to the point of being sacrilegious.

She was still thinking that when she set it aflame.

Cooper rolled ungracefully onto his back, his eyes fixed skyward, but not seeing anything there.

Do you see your children yet?

He did. He saw Tom, grinning, driving the truck for the first time—and younger, laughing as Donald swung him around in a circle out in front of the house, when there had still been a few scraps of lawn. Before the dust took over. Tom, holding the swaddled figure of Jesse, the grandchild he would never know—*could* never know, because the boy was years dead before Cooper had even known he existed.

And he saw Murph, a tiny, wrinkled thing in her mother's arms, a single curl of red hair on her otherwise bald pate. Murph, in the truck, pretending it was an Apollo lander, that the stick was the attitude or thrust controller, depending on what it needed to be at any point in her pretend flight.

Murph later, shifting the gears so he could drink his coffee.

And Murph in her bedroom, looking at the watch he had given her. He saw her throw it away, saw her tear-stained face.

Murph, he thought, as everything blurred. *I'm sorry.*

Murph gazed at the fire leaping through the corn, stalk to stalk, a living creature, gleeful in its life, as hungry as any new-born thing. Her disgust at what she had done was fading fast—it was the corn that was keeping Tom here, killing little Coop. If burning the corn—if giving the fire life—meant a new life for Coop and Lois, then it was well worth it. Tom would see the smoke. He would come. She didn't want to be here then.

She climbed back into the truck and headed out.

He would figure out who did it, soon enough. By then she would be long gone, and Lois and Coop along with her.

Brand watched as the cloudscape jetted by, as below them a huge plain opened up uninterrupted and white—except for what appeared to a be a tiny, broken doll lying near the edge of it, next to a deep blue hole.

"I see him," she told Case.

Cooper felt rather a hard thud on the ice, and at first thought it was nothing—just the last, random sensation of his dying body. But then he forced his eyes open and, through the wind-whipped ice and his own frozen tears, he saw it. The lander, and someone leaping out of it, elbow-thrusters firing.

Mann's come back to finish me off, he thought, trying to

summon the energy to crawl again. It was no use—his arms and legs might as well have been made of lead.

Then a moment later someone yanked his useless helmet off and he saw Brand's face through her own glass visor. She shoved something over his nose, and he was suddenly sucking in air—sweet, stale, canned air. That was all he wanted to do, breathe. She had to know.

Tars didn't seem to be having any luck with Kipp. He turned to Romilly.

"It needs a person to unlock its archival function," the robot informed him. He shifted a bit so Romilly could reach the data screen and start the procedure. Then he heard a voice—tiny, far off, shouting at him. He looked over and realized it was his helmet.

As he reached for it, Kipp stirred to life.

Romilly lifted the helmet, and the voice grew clearer. Identifiable.

"Brand?" he said. He was struck by how urgent she sounded.

But Romilly never heard the rest.

TWENTY-NINE

Mann struggled across the ice, trying to get his story straight in his mind. He would have to lose his own long-range transmitter, claim Cooper had accidently disengaged it in the fall when Mann had tried to save him.

Should've dropped it down the hole, he realized, but he wasn't going back there now.

He felt the shudder in the ice first, and then the sound and shock blew through him, frozen particles streaking past on the front of the concussion. At first he thought there had been some random shifting in the frozen masses and the ice had broken, but then he saw the black smoke churning from a nearby hilltop.

His hilltop. Where he'd lain so long in exile.

Where Kipp was.

He felt a fresh surge of terror. This was all spinning out of control.

"Dammit, Romilly," he muttered. He'd warned him, hadn't he? It wasn't his fault.

He switched his radio back on. Brand's voice greeted him.

"Come on, Cooper," she was saying. "Just a couple more steps…"

Well that tears it, he thought. He had known he would have to deal with Cooper, but he'd hoped to have the others as companions in the mission. *Desperately* hoped. He didn't want to be alone again. That was what had broken him, the solitude. If there was any thought that was intolerable, it was to be alone again.

But now he had no choice. There could be no mending this with Cooper. Romilly was certainly dead, and they would blame that on him, too.

Brand...

Still, he could hold onto the fact that this time it wouldn't be forever. There was still Edmunds' world, and plan B. He wouldn't be alone for the rest of his life. Wolf might still be alive, and there was no need for him to know anything about this... unpleasantness. And whether he survived or not, there would be the children. He could take the isolation again, as long as he knew there would be an end to it.

And maybe—once he had some leverage over her—he might be able to salvage Brand. Somehow. No one had a greater stake in this mission than she did. So that it might succeed, she might be made to see the realities.

Before he could appeal to her sense of reason, however, her sense of mission, he had to have the upper hand. Had to hold all of the cards.

He hurried toward the Ranger.

"Brand, I'm sorry," Cooper wheezed, as soon as the respirator was off of his face. "Mann lied—"

As he spoke, a look of comprehension swept across her face.

"Oh, no," she gasped.

* ✳ *

As Murph roared up to the house, Tom's truck was nowhere to be seen.

That was as planned—he would be fighting the fire she had set, trying to salvage the crop.

"Keep watch," she told Getty as she jerked the door open. Then she took off running toward the front door.

"Lois!" she called out as she hit the porch.

"There's been an explosion," Case informed them, as the lander rose and pivoted amid clouds of steam and frost.

"Where?" Brand asked.

"Dr. Mann's compound," he replied, as they leapt skyward.

Romilly, Cooper thought. *Tars*. Tars was with him.

What had Mann done to them?

Mann strapped into the Ranger, gave the systems a quick once-over, and then started the engines. As the ship shot into the air, he felt a sudden, unexpected exhilaration.

This planet had been his prison, and for most of the time he had believed it would be his tomb. It had made him do things he never thought himself capable of doing, and only now did he allow himself to understand how very much he despised it, the hold it had on him. It had been like a mirror held up to him, a mirror which showed him not his face, but his soul, and he hadn't liked what it showed him.

Yet accepting the darkness in his character was better than dying there. He could live with everything he had done, and everything he was going to do, so long as he didn't have to go back there. To that planet.

Which he didn't. It was all over now. Despite the odds, he had escaped. Wherever death finally caught up with him, it would not be on that icy tomb.

It felt good. Like a new start.

But he had to reach the *Endurance* before the others.

There was nothing to be seen of Mann's pod but billowing, oily black smoke, and Cooper knew Romilly was dead. Mann's story about Kipp had been pure bullshit—Kipp had collected data proving the planet was uninhabitable, and Mann had shut him down. He must have also booby-trapped him, in case anyone started prying.

Mann was Professor Brand's protégé, all right—a liar to the core. But the professor had justified his lies as necessary to save the human race—at least that was how he saw it. Mann had lied only to save himself. Cooper remembered Mann's comments about how the professor had made himself a monster, made the "ultimate sacrifice," to tell the world what it needed to be told.

Had Mann really been talking about himself? Was that how he justified all of this, in that diseased mind of his?

Romilly probably never felt a thing, Cooper thought. *Thank God.*

He and Brand watched the flames, both too sunken in despair to speak.

Suddenly something burst from the smoke. For a horrible moment he thought it was Romilly, burning to death, but then the figure resolved itself into the blocky machine that it was.

Tars.

Case turned the lander and opened the airlock. Tars leapt in with a dull *whump*. Then Case aimed the lander skyward. Only one thing mattered now, Cooper knew.

Who got to the *Endurance* first.

"Do you have a fix on the Ranger?" he asked Case.

"He's pushing into orbit," the robot replied.

"If he takes control of the ship, we're dead," Cooper said.

"He'd maroon us?" Brand asked. She seemed to be having trouble coming to terms with the recent behavior of NASA's best and brightest.

He remembered the conversation they'd had, before going into hypersleep. It seemed like a very long time ago.

"*Scientists, explorers,*" she had said. "*That's what I love. Out there we face great odds. Death. But not evil.*"

As if for some reason scientists and explorers were incapable of evil. *Cortez? Haber, the guy who invented chemical warfare?*

"*Just what we bring with us then,*" he had told her. Well, they had brought it.

The signs had been everywhere. Too bad he hadn't taken his own comment to heart. If he had exercised even a commonsense amount of suspicion, Romilly would still be alive. And they wouldn't be racing against hope.

"He *is* marooning us," Cooper said.

Lois loved Tom, but she had already lost one child, and she knew her son Coop was sick, and would only get sicker. So Murph didn't have a hard time convincing her what was best. Now she waited nervously as Lois gathered a few things for her and the boy.

Murph glanced up the stairs.

Would she ever come here again? It didn't seem likely, however this turned out. She wasn't sure she even wanted to come back. She remembered happy times here with her dad and brother, with Grandpa and—in her warmest, earliest memories—her mom.

The outside of the house had always looked worn, eroded away, its paint and wood stripped by relentless years of wind and dust. She remembered Grandpa—every day, twice a day, sweeping the porch, trying to keep the dust back. And it had worked—inside the house it had been safe. It had been home.

But now it seemed hollowed out. Maybe it had begun that night when she left her window open, inviting the dust into the house. Within a matter of days, her father had been gone, and nothing was ever right again.

Without Dad and Grandpa there, the house felt like someone she had once known well, but who was now in the last stages of Alzheimer's. A box that looked familiar, but wasn't, and never would be again.

And yet there was something she needed to do here. One last thing.

Without really thinking about it, she let her feet carry her up the stairs and through the doorway into her old room. She heard Lois and Coop, already outside with Getty, waiting, knowing that if Tom returned now, the whole plan was doomed.

But something, something told her she needed to be here, now—and not just for Lois and Coop.

"Come on, Murph!" she heard Getty shout. But the pull was like gravity.

She had to go.

As the lander roared toward the eternal night of space, Cooper moved up beside Case. His throat and nose still stung—for all he knew, the damage might be fatal. His lungs might be about to hemorrhage or whatever, and that would be that. For the moment, however, he was alive, and he was able, so it didn't make sense dwelling on the worst.

All that mattered was stopping Mann.

He hit the transmitter.

"Dr. Mann?" he said. "Dr. Mann, please respond."

There was no response. In a way, he was surprised. Mann seemed awfully fond of hearing himself talk, and almost psychotically desperate to justify himself. He must, Cooper guessed, have moved beyond the need for pretty speeches. He was concentrating on reaching the *Endurance*.

That was probably bad news—it meant that Mann had written them off. And he had too great a lead for them to catch up.

"He doesn't know the docking procedure," Case pointed out.

"The autopilot does," Cooper replied, thinking about how screwed they were. There was simply no way to beat him there…

"Not since Tars disabled it," Case said.

Cooper looked over to the airlock and the singed robot that occupied it. He felt a blaze of newfound respect.

"Nice," he said "What's your trust setting?"

"Lower than yours, apparently," Tars replied.

"Dr. Mann?" Cooper's voice came again. Mann ignored him. What point would there be in answering him? Instead he studied the navigation panel.

"Dr. Mann, if you attempt docking—"

Mann switched off the receiver. What he didn't need now was any sort of distraction. Not when he was this close.

* ❉ *

Murph looked around her old room, the room that had once been her mother's. The bookshelves that had spoken to her. Would they speak to her again? Was her ghost still here?

She waited, but the books remained in their places.

Murph spotted the box of her stuff. Cautiously, as if she feared it might contain a snake, she went to it and looked inside.

THIRTY

Mann breathed a sigh of relief as he came up on the *Endurance*. According to his instruments, he had a significant lead on the lander, giving him plenty of time to secure his position. He drew up to the larger ship, and then switched on the autopilot so it could finish the tricky business of docking.

"Auto-docking sequence withheld," the computer said.

Mann blinked at the screen. Why on earth would the docking sequence be withheld?

"Override," he told the machine.

"Unauthorized," the computer answered.

Well, that was a problem. He didn't know the sequence himself—he hadn't been trained for this. But with the Ranger coming up behind, it didn't look like he had a choice.

He had to do it manually.

As they climbed into orbit, Cooper could see Mann was in position to dock, but that wasn't as easy as it might appear. The ring ship wasn't spinning, but it was still moving in orbit, and Mann had to match that. Getting a general velocity match wasn't a problem, but it couldn't just be in the ball park.

He tried the transmitter again.

"Dr. Mann, do *not* attempt docking," he said. "Dr. Mann?"

Static was his only reply.

Mann knew he had the closest thing he was going to get to a synchronic orbit, so he left the controls and went quickly to the airlock, which was fast lining up with a hatch on the *Endurance*. He began working the mechanical grapple, seeking to grip the other ship and keep the two airlocks aligned so they could be coupled.

It was working. The ships bumped together. He was starting a sigh of relief when the computer spoke up again.

"Imperfect contact," it said. "Hatch lockout."

Mann paused, thinking furiously.

How perfect does the latch need to be? he wondered. *All it has to do is hold together for a few seconds.* That was all the time it would take for him to cross. Then he could seal up from the other side. If he had to cut the Ranger loose — well, there was a spare, and another lander, as well. He might lose a little air in the process, sure, yet there would still be plenty, and he would be the only person on board.

He needed to get on board *now*. The lead he had built was quickly diminishing.

"Override," he commanded.

"Hatch lockout disengaged," the computer informed him.

Thank God. He was starting to think he was locked out of everything.

He drifted toward the airlock controls.

* ❋ *

So close…

Cooper stared at the joined ships.

Looks like the sonofabitch did it, he thought.

"Is he locked on?" Cooper demanded, knowing Case had a running telemetry feed from the *Endurance*.

"Imperfectly,' Case replied.

Cooper grabbed the transmitter.

"Dr. Mann!" he yelped desperately. "Dr. Mann! Do not, repeat, do not open the hatch. If you—"

Mann looked at the grapples. They were opening and closing, trying to complete the seal, but he knew he didn't have time to get it perfect. The lander was almost there, and if he lost the partial lock he already had, he might drift off and have to start over again, which would be a disaster. Cooper doubtless knew the docking sequence, and he had both robots at his disposal. He would dock easily, and then he would be in control.

That was *not* going to happen.

"What happens if he blows the hatch?" Cooper asked Case.

"Nothing good,' Case replied.

He considered the tableau. Would Mann go through with it?

Crap—of course he will, Cooper knew. Mann wasn't really a pilot—Kipp had taken care of that. But whatever flight training the scientist had been through, it wouldn't have included the skills needed for manual docking. There wouldn't have been any call for it at any point during the Lazarus mission.

Cooper, on the other hand, had it drilled into him—over and over—that you never, *ever* open the locks without a perfect seal. Whatever his merits, Mann was—like the rest of them—a theory man. If he thought through the physics of opening the hatch, he probably wouldn't take the chance—but he wasn't thinking about that now. His only goal was to get onto the *Endurance*, and fast.

"Pull us back!" Cooper ordered.

Case hit the thrusters, and the *Endurance* began to dwindle in their windscreen.

Then there was silence. Cooper realized he was hardly breathing.

"Case," Brand said, snapping out of it. "Relay my transmission to his onboard computer, and have it rebroadcast as emergency P.A."

Finally, Cooper thought. Brand was back in the game. That was good, because he sure as hell needed her.

"Dr. Mann," Brand said. "Do not open the in—"

Mann was reaching for the lever to release the inner hatch when Brand's voice suddenly burst from the computer.

"*—peat*," she said. "*Do not open inner hatch!*"

Startled, he moved over to the transmitter and switched it on.

"Brand," he said, "I don't know what Cooper's told you, but I'm taking control of the *Endurance*, then we'll talk about continuing the mission. This is not your survival, or Cooper's—this is about mankind's."

He turned back and pulled the lever.

THIRTY-ONE

It all happened in silence, of course, and at distance, so to Cooper it seemed unreal. It was as if he was watching some of his model spaceships, suspended on fishing line in front of a star field.

First he saw a flare of flame and then a cloud puff from the spot where the two ships were joined, followed by a steady stream of white vapor. He didn't need to ask what it was—it was air gushing out from both the Ranger and *Endurance*, crystallizing almost instantly in the vacuum of space.

The loss of air was a problem, but the secondary affect was a disaster. The air in both ships was pressurized at around twelve pounds per square inch, so it was jetting out with enough velocity to act like a steering rocket. As Cooper watched, aghast, the angle of the air stream began turning the wheel that was *Endurance*—ponderously at first, but with gathering speed, like a pinwheel firework on the Fourth of July. He watched the partially joined airlocks twist and shatter, and then the Ranger was ripped away, tearing itself apart in the process and rupturing one of the *Endurance*'s modules as it went. Venting more air to freeze in the void, adding more thrust to the ship's spin.

As it spun, the ghostly hand of planetary gravity took over and the great ship began dropping ponderously toward the frozen planet below.

"Oh, my God," Brand said.

Cooper got behind the controls and took the sticks, firing the thrusters. He dove beneath the crippled starship, dodging the debris from the Ranger.

"Cooper," Case said, "there's no point in using our fuel to—"

"Just analyze the *Endurance*'s spin," he said, cutting Case short.

"What are you doing?" Brand asked.

"Docking," Cooper replied.

He pushed the thrusters, trying to match the larger ship's rotation.

"*Endurance* rotation sixty-seven, sixty-eight rotations per minute," Case informed him.

"Get ready to match it on the retro thrusters," Cooper said.

"It's not possible," Case argued.

"No," Cooper said, grimly. "It's *necessary*."

He noticed that the *Endurance* was shedding bits of itself, sending them spinning off into the void..

"*Endurance* is hitting atmosphere," Case remarked.

"She's got no heat shield!" Brand said.

Cooper maneuvered beneath the spinning wheel, only feet from the starship. The airlock was there, and relative to the downward fall of the *Endurance*, the lander was more-or-less motionless.

But that wasn't even halfway where they needed to be. The dock was whirling around at incredible speed. Speed they were going to have to match.

"Case, you ready?" he asked.

"Ready." Case replied.

Cooper looked again at *Endurance*, and felt a blink coming on. Maybe Case was right. They still had the lander. With it they might manage to limp home. Probably not, but maybe. Yet if this failed, it was all over. They were all dead.

"Cooper," Case said, "this is no time for caution."

Cooper felt a smile on his face.

Right.

"If I black out," he said, "Take the stick. Tars, get ready to engage the docking mechanism Brand—hold tight."

"*Endurance* is starting to heat—" Case said.

"Hit it!" Cooper told him.

He felt the retros fire, and the lander started to spin, picking up speed quickly as both ships streaked toward the waiting ice below. The g-forces increased, as well, pushing them against their restraints, trying to crush them. Cooper felt the blood rushing away from his head, and struggled to remain conscious.

They weren't falling cleanly anymore. The atmosphere was pushing back, and hard, bouncing and yawing the tiny ship. Mann's planet seemed to be everywhere, and the curve of its horizon was fast straightening out.

He saw Tars open the airlock. The *Endurance* was still spinning relative to them, but slowly, as they neared matching the rpm. After several heart-stopping moments they lined up, and Tars fired the grapple—but they hit an air pocket—the hatches went out of line and the grapple caught nothing.

He glanced over, saw Brand had passed out, and knew he wasn't far behind her. He fastened his eyes on his instruments rather than the wild whirling vista of Mann's planet that was moving into and out of view. He tried to hold on.

"Come on Tars," he said. "Come on…"

Cooper heard the grapple fire again, and the ship suddenly lurched, violently.

"Got it!" Tars announced.

Immediately Case reversed the direction of the thrust and their rotation began to slow.

"Gen—gentle, Case," Cooper muttered, half out of it.

Mann's planet began rotating into view less frequently, just once every few seconds, until finally they were barely turning at all.

"Getting ready to pull us up," Cooper said.

But it might already be too late. They were still falling, and *Endurance* was starting to burn in earnest, parts melting and sloughing off of her, becoming meteorites that streaked into the atmosphere.

Cooper eased on the main thrusters, fearful of breaking her up.

"Come on," he said. "You can do it…"

The powerful engine began to slow their fall, but they were so close, so deep in the atmosphere…

The moments stretched, as if they were once again in the grip of the black hole—as if hours or days were dragging by, rather than just a handful of crucial seconds. Cooper felt their fall slow almost glacially, then stop.

And then—finally, painfully, they started back up out of the gravity well that was Mann's world. The horizon dropped away behind them. Only then daring to breathe, Cooper pulled back on the sticks and allowed himself a silent moment of triumph.

Brand stirred. Cooper turned to Case, allowing himself a real smile.

"Right." he said. "And now for our next trick…"

"It'll have to be good," Case informed him. "We're heading into Gargantua's pull."

Dammit! Cooper thought. Some days there just weren't

enough doors to slam. He unbuckled his harness.

"Take her," he told Case.

The *Endurance* was a mess inside. Everything that could tear loose had done so, along with a few things that supposedly couldn't. Without gravity, the debris swirled around crazily kicked everywhere by jets of steam and air from as-yet unpatched ruptures in the ship's hull and fluid circulatory systems.

Case and Tars went to deal with the worst of those, while he and Brand took inventory of the rest of the ship.

So far as Cooper could tell, the population bomb was still intact and functional. Brand would do a more thorough analysis later. Personally, he found he hated the sight of the thing. It might mean life for the human race, but it represented the death of his children. In fact, it was more than that. The human race was more than a collection of solitary biological organisms. It was the end result of a million years of existence as a species—a million years of stories, myths, relationships, ideas both important and nonsensical, poetry, philosophy, engineering—science.

Being human was to inherit from a parent, a sibling, a family, a community, a town, a culture, a civilization. Humans hadn't just been biological objects since before they became human.

Sure, he and Brand could bring a few thousand biologically human entities into existence with this thing, but could the two of them really substitute for the immense web of heritage, affiliation—love? Was that really saving the human race? Salvaging a single seed from a forest before it was burnt to the ground didn't mean you had saved the forest. You could never replicate its baroque, unique ecosystem. Unfreezing human embryos was not going to "save" the human race.

The human race as he knew it was going to die. Whatever came out of this machine, it would be something different. Maybe better, maybe worse—but not the same.

Case was flagging for his attention.

"We're slipping towards Gargantua," the mechanical informed him. "Shall I use the main engines?"

"No!" Cooper said, firmly. "Let her slide as long as we can." He had been thinking about this. He couldn't be sure of everything until he had a fine-tuned sense of their status, but he knew already that fighting Gargantua wasn't going to get them anywhere.

He pushed off and flew to where Tars was welding a bulkhead.

"Give it to me," he said.

"There's good news and bad news," Tars began.

"I've heard that, Tars," he replied. "Just give it to me straight."

Amelia felt a shiver of dread as Cooper came in. It seemed as if they were trapped in a loop of disasters, one after another. Whatever news he might have, the odds were it couldn't be good.

She had been trying to stay occupied with the particulars of her duties—primarily making certain that they could still implement plan B. The population bomb had been roughed up enough that she'd needed to overhaul the cryonics, which she had managed to accomplish with a little help from Case. It was a makeshift fix that required cannibalizing Romilly's cryo-bed, but then again, he wasn't going to need it. Once they made planetfall, she could use some parts of the *Endurance* they still needed to rig a more reliable system. They couldn't thaw all of the embryos at once—the bomb would need to continue working for decades, at least.

She wondered how many children she and Cooper would be able to manage, now that it was just the two of them. Five? Ten?

At least he had some experience along those lines.

You want a big family, Coop? It was going to be an odd conversation to have. *Probably a painful one, too—at least for him.*

It all might simply be moot, anyway—the *Endurance* might not be able to take them *anywhere*, given the damage she had suffered. And even if she could, what if Edmunds' planet was no better than the others?

What if "they"—whoever the mysterious architects were—had been playing a cruel joke all along? Or, perhaps worse, hadn't possessed any real concept of what human beings needed when it came to settling a new home?

If the average person were asked to find a new environment suitable for the chemosynthetic bacteria that lived around deep-sea thermal vents, would they know where to start? And would the difference between such bacteria and *Homo sapiens* be significant to beings who lived in five dimensions and spoke with gravity? Perhaps not. Some life from Earth would live just fine on either Miller's planet or Mann's.

Just not human life. And if they were wrong about two planets—no, strike that—eleven planets, counting those visited by Lazarus astronauts who had found their systems completely wanting—why shouldn't they be wrong about *all* of them? If they really knew what they were doing, why couldn't they have pointed humanity to the one right world for them?

But then she remembered the distorted image in the ship as they passed through the wormhole,—and she couldn't bring herself to believe that there was any sort of deception involved. And she still had faith in Wolf, in his planet—believed everything she had said that day, trying to persuade Cooper and Romilly that their best course was the one that led to his world.

Edmunds' planet was where they needed to be. They just had to get there. Which, to her, no longer seemed likely.

She waited for what Cooper had come to say.

He stopped within arm's reach of her. They were both sealed in their spacesuits, yet it felt very—personal.

"The navigation mainframe's destroyed," he said, "And we don't have enough life support to make it back to Earth.

"But..." he added, "We might scrape to Edmunds' planet."

So much had gone wrong that Amelia accepted his words with genuine caution. She tried to read his tone, his expression. She knew this had to be devastating for him, and the relief—no, happiness—that threatened to overwhelm her had to be kept in check. She couldn't let him see it. Wolf might be alive, or he might be dead. But to know, to know for certain—there was freedom in that.

There was closure, which she desperately needed. If she was to move on with plan B—if that was to be the sum of her remaining life, she needed to know. And if she was wrong about Edmunds' world—well then, they were done. One way or another, their journey would finally be over. For her, that would be closure of another sort.

As for Cooper, she knew in her heart that no possible outcome would bring him solace. That tinged her inner elation with sadness.

"What about fuel?" she asked, trying to stick to the practical aspects of the situation, to keep her emotions at bay.

"Not enough," Cooper said. He smiled. "But I've got a plan. Let Gargantua suck us right to her horizon—then a powered slingshot around to launch us at Edmunds." He explained it so easily that he might as well have been talking about taking a ride in a pickup truck. *Sure, I'll just spin the wheel around like this, and downshift 'er...*

Yet she knew it wasn't that easy.

"Manually?" Amelia questioned. Cooper had shown that he was a great pilot, but he was still only human. To slingshot around a black hole—without the mainframe? The tiniest mistake would see them dragged through Gargantua's horizon and into its singularity.

"That's what I'm here for," Cooper said confidently. "I'll take us just inside the critical orbit." He said it like he expected her to believe him, and to her surprise, she realized she did. He could do it. And if he couldn't—well, what the hell. They probably wouldn't feel a thing, anyway.

"And the time slippage?" she asked softly.

His mouth turned in a melancholy little smile, and she saw traces of his grief.

"Neither of us can afford to worry about relativity right now," he said, and she saw something else in his expression. A sort of tranquility, as if in his sorrow he had found some kind of peace.

"I'm sorry Cooper," she said, and hardly thinking about it, she reached to embrace him. They were both in spacesuits, of course, so there was little physical sensation, but it still felt natural. They touched their faceplates together, and the moment seemed to linger.

THIRTY-TWO

Once again they fell toward the Gargantua's yawning nothingness. In the remaining Ranger, Cooper sat sorting himself, preparing. He watched as Tars separated the lander from the battered *Endurance*.

He wished he'd had a few more moments with his children. Every second, gold in his hand.

The slingshot effect was nothing new. Comets had been doing it since stars were formed. As for humans, it had been used almost as long as there had been interplanetary travel. *Mariner 10* had been the first to employ it, sending the unmanned spacecraft past Venus to explore Mercury, followed by *Voyager* and *Galileo*.

You basically sent a spacecraft falling toward a much bigger body—say, a planet. The craft picked up speed as it "fell" toward the planet, whipped around it in a very tight pass, and then used the speed it had gained falling toward the planet to escape its gravitational pull, moving on a very different trajectory. And since the planet was in motion, the spacecraft could pick up the planet's orbital speed, adding it to its own velocity. In this way you both changed course and increased speed toward another, final target without ever having burned an ounce of fuel.

That was what Cooper intended to do with Gargantua.

Of course, Gargantua wasn't a planet, or even—in the conventional sense—a star. And if it hadn't been—as Romilly put it—a "gentler" black hole, they would never have had a chance.

As Romilly had said—and as his twenty-odd years of notes had meticulously measured and elucidated—Gargantua rotated, which meant that it dragged space-time along for the ride. A slingshot was entirely plausible, but a bit more… complicated than zipping near a planet.

Cooper checked everything for the umpteenth time, hoping Romilly hadn't gone more than a little looney while he was alone. Because Gargantua wasn't going to grant him the slightest clemency for even the tiniest mistake.

Back in the *Endurance*, Amelia watched the lander come loose and shift orientation as Cooper and Tars prepared the maneuver.

Cooper's voice came over the radio.

"Once we've gathered enough speed around Gargantua, we use Lander One and Ranger Two as rocket boosters to push us out of the black hole's gravity," he explained, as the lander reattached in the rear of the ring module, blocking her view of the Ranger and Cooper.

"The linkages between landers are destroyed," Cooper said. *"So we'll control manually. When Lander One's fuel is spent, Tars will detach—"*

"—and get sucked into the black hole," Tars finished.

Amelia thought they were joking at first. They did a lot of that, Tars and Cooper. Sometimes she wanted to change the humor settings on *both* of them. But it crept over her that this time there wasn't any humor involved.

"Why does he have to detach?" she asked.

"We have to shed mass if we're gonna escape that gravity," Cooper explained.

"Newton's third law," Tars put in. *"The only way humans have ever figured out of getting somewhere is to leave something behind."*

Doyle, Amelia thought, *Romilly, Mann, her father—and now Tars?* How much loss could she take?

"Cooper," she said, feeling a little desperate, and even a little indignant. "You can't ask Tars to do this for us—"

"He's a robot, Amelia," Cooper shot back. *"I don't have to ask him to do anything."*

"Cooper," she snapped. "You asshole!"

"Sorry," Cooper said. *"You broke up a little over there."*

She was ready to launch into a full-blown tirade, but Tars interceded

"It's what we intended, Dr. Brand," Tars said. *"It's our last chance to save people on Earth. If we can find some way to transmit the quantum data I'll find in there, they might still make it."* The robot's calm, reasonable tone checked her anger.

"If there's someone still there to receive it," she allowed, feeling emptier than ever.

Was it possible? Did it even make sense? It was hard to know anymore. But it was a better chance than nothing, and Cooper was probably right about shedding mass. Maddeningly, he was seldom wrong about such things.

But if there was a way to prove her father wrong, to redeem plan A, they had to take it. It just seemed so wrong that Tars had to be the one to make the sacrifice. It should be her, but it was too late for that—Cooper had seen to it, she realized. And—to be fair—neither the robots nor

Cooper knew enough about the population bomb. If glitches developed, if improvisation was required, she had to be there. Seen logically, it should be Tars who did this, and not her.

But it was still hard to watch from safety as someone else paid her bills.

As the engines pushed them forward, ever faster, the ship began to shudder.

Amelia tightened her harness and tried not to revisit what would happen if Cooper was even slightly wrong in his calculations. They were so close now that all she could see was a massive Stygian ocean wreathed in golden, glowing gas. It seemed impossible they were going to escape as they fell, faster and faster, that this ancient dead god would let them slip his greedy, immortal grasp. Nothing as frail and mortal as the *Endurance* stood a chance in the face of such cosmic hunger. Even if they made it past perigee—their nearest approach to the black hole—they would surely break up on the way out.

But she had to believe—had to believe that Cooper could pull it off.

And, so suddenly, they were there, at the bottom of their fall. At least she *hoped* it was the bottom.

"Maximum velocity achieved," Case announced. *"Prepare to fire escape thrusters."*

"Ready," Tars said.

"Ready," Cooper echoed.

Amelia couldn't tear her eyes from the impossible horizon, the black-hearted monster that lay below them.

"Main engine ignition in three, two, one, mark," Case intoned.

The hull thrummed as the main engines fired, adding to the inertia already whipping them around Gargantua, turning the black hole's gravity against it in a demonstration of stellar jujitsu. But the giant wasn't giving up without a fight. *Endurance* strained to its limits for freedom, like a four-wheel drive trying to climb out of a sandy hole with the wheels spinning and the slope sliding backward.

Inertia wasn't enough. Nor were the main engines.

More thrust was needed.

"*Lander One*," Case continued, "*engines on my mark… three, two, one,* mark—"

"*Fire*," Tars said, and the lander's engines engaged. The *Endurance* protested even more, her metal skeleton audibly straining as the small craft emptied it fuel reserves in one massive, maximum burn.

"*Ranger Two, engines on my mark*," Case said. "*Three, two, one,* mark."

"*Fire*," she heard Cooper say.

Amelia saw the stars again as they pulled away from Gargantua, toward the grand spectacle of the night sky, so much brighter than that of the solar system. And somewhere out there—outshone by nebulae and pulsars and blaze of the stellar newborn—there was the faint red dot for which they were aiming.

Edmunds' planet.

Unbelievably, the powered slingshot seemed to be working. The tipping point was still ahead, but they were approaching it.

"*That little maneuver cost us fifty-one years*," Cooper reported.

"You don't sound bad for a hundred and twenty," Amelia responded, a little giddy with reaction.

"*Lander One, prepare to detach on my mark*," Case said. "*Three…*"

She could see the lander, Tars at the controls, and her brief cheerfulness vanished as quickly as it had come. The lander's fuel was spent, and now it was just dead weight. As was Tars.

Space required a certain parsimony of thought. Something was either useful, or it was dead weight, and if it was dead weight you dropped it. They had been shedding weight since the first stage booster detached while they were still in Earth's atmosphere. Like Tars said, you had to leave something behind.

Was that how her father had felt about Earth, and the rest of the human race? Were they dead weight that had to be dropped, so that a handful could move on?

But Tars wasn't dead weight.

Tars was Tars. He had a humor setting…

"*Two one*, mark," Case said.

Through the cockpit window, she saw Tars moving.

"*Detach*," he said.

And the lander dropped away.

"Goodbye, Tars," she said.

"*See you on the other side, Coop*," Tars said optimistically.

Amelia frowned. What was that supposed to mean? Something about the way had Tars said it…

The lander had spent its velocity and begun to fall toward the black hole.

"*Case?*" she heard Cooper say. "*Nice reckless flying.*"

"*Learned from the master*," the robot replied. The Ranger's engines sputtered and went out as it, too, exhausted its fuel.

"*Ranger Two*," Case said, "*prepare to detach.*"

For an instant she thought she had misheard, but then she looked up at Cooper's face and the faint apology written on it.

"No!" she shouted, grasping for the buckles of her harness.

"*On my mark,*" Case said.

Free of the restraint, she pushed herself to the window, staring at Cooper, pleading with her eyes.

"What are you doing?" she demanded.

"*Newton's third law,*" he said. "*You have to leave something behind.*"

"...*two...*" Case said.

She pushed her faceplate against the window, trying to somehow bridge the vacuum separating them.

"You told me we had enough resources for both of us!" she said.

"...*one,*" Case continued.

Cooper smiled at her fondly.

"*Hey,*" he told her. "*We agreed—ninety percent.*"

"*Mark,*" Case said.

She saw him reach for the button, watching through the jewels of her tears, forming perfect orbs inside her helmet, drifting, collecting in her eyelashes.

He looked at her one last time, then hit the button.

"*De—*" he began, and he swallowed. "*Detach.*"

And the Ranger—and Cooper—were gone.

THIRTY-THREE

Cooper watched the *Endurance*'s main drive diminish to a star-like point of light as the ship accelerated away from Gargantua, and he fell toward the massive dead blackness. His breath quickened as he wondered what it was going to feel like—if it was going to feel like anything at all, for that matter.

He peered at the horizon, at the distorted light of the last stars—the last light—he thought, that he would ever see. Glancing upward, however, he saw the universe as if through a circular window, a porthole opening onto infinity.

There is a beauty to this, he thought, as he watched a glowing plasma jet stream across his field of view. He had never known he could hold terror in one hand and wonder in the other with such perfect balance. And indeed, as the fall sped up, terror began to overbalance a bit.

Trying to keep from hyperventilating, Cooper turned the Ranger down, gasping at the flare of the horizon.

"Tars?" he asked. "Are you there?"

His only answer was static as he watched the lander nose down into the black.

Then Cooper realized he was losing his fight with panic. He'd hoped to go out with some dignity, but now it was all he could do not to scream.

Far above, Amelia heard Cooper's breathing. It was becoming louder and louder. Crying, she balled her fists so tight her nails cut into her palms.

And then, abruptly—as his harsh breaths rose toward a crescendo—the radio dimmed out and fell silent.

She stared out into space, the last surviving human crew of the *Endurance*. Gargantua still filled her field of vision, but every breath she took put thousands of miles between her and the black hole.

For a long time she could not look away. But at last—as she knew she must—Amelia turned from her grief, from what lay behind her, and looked ahead to the distant red orb that was now her destination.

Looking toward hope.

"It's totally black," Cooper said, knowing probably no one could hear him. "No light at all." He paused. "Brand? Can you hear me?"

Murph stood in her room, the ruddy light of dusk fading beyond the window pane.

She sat on the bed and looked into the box. She took out the model of the lunar lander, remembering a little ruefully how she had punched that kid for saying the Apollo missions were faked—but even now, not really regretting it or the larger fistfight that followed.

She looked up at the books.

"Come on Murph!" she heard Getty yell from outside. "We don't have much time."

Cooper saw something coming out of the darkness, something glittering and white, like a handful of sand cast by a giant into a whirlwind. As the Ranger plunged into it, it streamed by like glowing diamonds, like sleet seen through high-beams. It was beautiful and terrifying, becoming more the latter as it began to beat against his hull. The entire ship shuddered as the hail became more like red-hot rivers, shredding the Ranger to pieces.

"Fuel cell overload," his computer informed him. "Destruction imminent. Initiate ejection."

Into that? his inner voice squeaked. But he didn't have a choice in the matter, and for the second time in his life he saw the controls ripped involuntarily from his hands, and he was blown out of the Ranger as it broke into a line of explosions running down the infinite rabbit hole, with him right behind. And then Cooper finally screamed, because his mind couldn't take it, and all that was left was the part of him that couldn't think but could only react, the part as old as the first primate, the first mammal, the first water-bound worm with a notochord.

Then, without warning, something like a great invisible hand seemed to take him, pull him to the side, away from the stream of debris. And toward—something. Something that somehow didn't seem to belong here. A grid of some sort—an infinite series of cubbyholes, each square opening nearly identical...

No, not cubbyholes—tunnels, he realized, as without slowing in the slightest he hurtled feet first into one, banging painfully into the side. Still hollering, he began kicking at whatever the walls were made of, and felt some of it give, slowing his fall. It was as if the passage was made of unmortared bricks. It was weirdly familiar, and nothing like what he'd thought he would find in a black hole.

He kicked again, and added his arms and it gave even more. At the same time he sloughed off more of his forward momentum.

He kept at it and slowed further, coming, at last, thankfully, to a stop. For the moment, all was finally calm — no more falling, no more motion at all — just floating in a strange space that seemed more familiar each moment. He had time to wonder if he was dead, or dreaming, or just stuck at the event horizon of the black hole, frozen in time, his mind playing out weird fantasies as it would for the rest of time.

Putting aside the possibilities that he was dead or dreaming — he couldn't do anything if either was true — he reached out to the wall of the passage. If this was actually happening, then where the hell was he? How could a trans-dimensional space inside of a black hole be made of bricks?

But they didn't look like bricks.. For one thing, they were thinner than most bricks, and not as dense. Each had two thick outer edges enclosing hundreds of much thinner lines, like paper...

Like books...

If you were on the wall side of a bookshelf. And from each book streamed a ghostly line of light, as if each book had left a trail. The light created a vast matrix around him, going off in all directions.

He pushed at one of the objects, and it shifted incrementally. He pushed harder, and then harder until finally it popped through and dropped out of sight.

Peering through the gap he saw her. She was ten and her hair was wet. She had a towel around her neck, and she was just turning, startled by the book falling.

"Murph?" he called. "Murph?"

But she didn't react. She just stood there, gazing at the shelves, at the book on the floor, which he could no longer see. Then she came cautiously toward the shelf and bent down. When she came up she was holding a broken toy.

The lunar lander.

In the twilight, Murph turned the lander model in her hand, remembering, wondering. Outside, Getty was sounding more frantic. But she felt somehow, there was something here.

Cooper watched his ten-year-old daughter examine the broken model.

"Murph!" He tried again. "Murph!"

But she still didn't hear him. She turned and left the room, and he knew where she was going—to the breakfast table, where he would chastise her for being unscientific and not taking care of "our stuff."

Desperately, he looked around and realized that he was in something like a cube, and each wall of the cube looked into Murph's room from a different angle, as if the room had been turned inside out, reversed, and put back together. And it wasn't just the one room, the one bookshelf. He saw now the matrix of light held multiple iterations of the room, maybe infinite, tunnels and passages going in every direction, framed, held together by the light streaming from the books, the walls, the objects in the room.

It was disorienting, and he wished Romilly was there to explain to him what was going on. He had to be operating in more than three dimensions, but since his mind was only built to handle three — well, he figured it was doing its best.

He was still in free-fall. By floating around and using his thrusters, he could effectively move to each iteration of Murph's room, so he pulled himself to the next one and punched out two more books.

Through the resulting gap he saw an empty bedroom. It didn't stay empty for long, though. The door opened and — well — *he* walked in. His younger self, looking bothered about something. A moment later, Murph entered as well.

Cooper slammed into the books, kicked another out, furiously determined to get their attention.

Murph rubbed her hand across the old desk, remembering all those years ago when she had pushed it in front of the door, how angry and sad she had been. She reached for the chair, too, and tilted it back.

Cooper watched Murph put the chair on top of the desk, completing her barricade of the door. A moment later, he saw it move a little as someone — no, not someone, but him, the earlier him — began to nudge through.

"Just go," Murph said. "If you're leaving — just leave now."

Cooper spun around to another wall, and saw his earlier self on the other side of the door.

"Don't go, you idiot!" he yelled, as the other Cooper closed the door. Going to let Murph cool off. Precisely the wrong move. "Don't leave your kids, you goddamn fool!" he shouted.

He began punching at the walls with everything in him, but not blindly. He knew what to do.

"S," he said. "T…"

Murph was watching now. She didn't look scared. She looked amazed, excited, interested.

"A," he grunted. "Y."

He stopped to catch his breath, then watched in frustration as his earlier self reached through the cracked door and around, to lift off the chair so he could push back the desk and enter the room.

"Stay, you idiot!" he yelled. "Tell him, Murph! Stay…"

He watched numbly as it played out, just like before. He gave her the watch. She hurled it across the room.

"Murph," he pleaded. "Tell him again! Don't let him leave…"

He broke down and began to cry, the sheer frustration of having to watch it all, and not be able to do anything. It was way too much to handle. Once again, he wondered if he was dead. If this was Hell.

Because it damn sure felt like it.

Murph picked up her old notebook and paged through it, stopping when she reached her Morse code interpretation of the gaps in the books.

Stay.

She looked up from the notebook back to the books, and felt something almost like a rush of wind go through her, as if some hidden place had suddenly been opened. She went to the shelves, and began pulling books out.

The smell of burning corn drifted up from downstairs, where the door stood open for her.

"Murph," Cooper sobbed. "Don't let me leave."

But his earlier self turned, heading for the door.

"Stay!" he screamed, slamming the books with all of his might. One dropped, and the earlier Cooper turned. Looked at it...

And left.

Cooper put his head against the books, weeping.

Murph stared at the gaps she had made in the books, and then back at her notebook. Her throat tightened.

"Dad," she said. "It was you. You were my ghost..."

Tears started, not from pain or anger or sadness, but from the greatest joy she had felt in many, many years. He hadn't abandoned her. He had tried. He had been her ghost all along.

Cooper was still crying when he heard his name. He turned, but there was no one there, and he realized the voice had come from his radio. He also recognized the voice.

Tars.

"You survived," Cooper said.

"*Somewhere,*" Tars agreed. "*In their fifth dimension. They saved us.*"

"Who's 'they'?" he asked. "And why would they help us?"

"*I don't know,*" Tars admitted, "*but they constructed this three-dimensional space inside their five-dimensional reality, to allow you to understand it.*"

"It isn't working!" Cooper exploded.

"*Yes, it is,*" Tars said. "*You've seen that time here is represented as a physical dimension. You even worked out that you can exert a force across space-time.*"

Cooper frowned, trying to understand. And then, suddenly, he did. The streams of light from the books were paths. Through time. Showing where each thing in Murph's room had come from and where it was going. And the force he was exerting...

"Gravity," he said. "To send a message..."

He looked around the infinite tunnels, the infinite Murphs, the lines from the books, the shelves, everything in the room going off as far as he could see in any and every direction.

"Gravity crosses the dimensions, including time," he said.

When he pressed an icon on a control panel, it wasn't the icon that made the ship move. It was just something that translated his intention to the mechanisms that could actually start the ship. Similarly, although it felt as if he was punching the books out with his fists and feet, in fact that was not possible. His physical body, *this* physical body was not—could not be—in the past.

But gravity could. Like Tars said, gravity cut across and through all of the dimensions. When he punched at one of them, what he was really doing was sending a pulse through space-time, a gravitic surge that was responsible for moving the books.

In other words, he was the source of a gravitational anomaly, and "they" had given him control of it in the most natural way possible—by making his sense of self, his sense of body, the controller. By giving images—icons—that he could understand and exert that force upon.

He realized suddenly that there might be a point to this. Something beyond watching himself make the biggest mistake of his life, over and over again. He just had to understand the tools he had been given, and determine what to do with them.

He pulled himself back to the wall and started counting books.

"You have the quantum data now," Cooper said to Tars.

"*I'm transmitting it on all wavelengths,*" Tars confirmed, "*but nothing's getting out.*"

"I can do it..." Cooper breathed.

He reached for one of the timelines—*worldlines, really*, he mused—and plucked at it. To his delight, a wave ran up the line, like a guitar string vibrating, affecting that book slightly, wherever and whenever it was.

"*Such complicated data,*" Tars said. "*Sending it to a child...*"

"Not just any child," Cooper said.

Murph stood in the darkening room, looking at her notebook, puzzling at it. She knew there must be more now. An answer...

Her father had been here, as the ghost.

Where is he now?

"Murph!" Getty hollered, sounding more frantic than ever. "Come on!"

THIRTY-FOUR

Cooper saw Murph staring out the window, and knew his earlier self was driving away. Toward NASA, the *Endurance*—this.

"Even if you communicate it here," Tars reasoned, *"she wouldn't recognize its significance for years..."*

He began to become angry. After all the fear and frustration, the feelings that burned up through him provided a welcome change.

"Then figure something out!" he snapped. "Everybody on Earth is going to die!"

"Cooper," Tars said, *"They didn't bring us here to change the past."*

Of course they didn't. Cooper paused, calming himself. No, he couldn't change the past. But there was something else... something about what Tars was saying.

They didn't bring us here to change the past.

They...

"We brought ourselves here," he said, and he pushed off, found another angle, saw the room in a slightly different moment. It was full of dust from the storm, the storm that had come upon them at the baseball game.

Murph had left her window open…

"Tars," he said, studying the dust. "Feed me the coordinates of NASA in binary."

And with his fingers, he traced the pattern, the lines he had found after the dust storm—

She ran her finger along the windowsill and examined the dust on it, remembering the pattern on the floor that day, how happy she was that she had been vindicated, that her father believed her. Sort of. But he had never believed all of it. Only the part he *wanted* to believe, that part that said he had been chosen to go into space. The ghost he had discounted.

And yet he *was* the ghost. Both. Giving himself the coordinates that would lead him to NASA, but also telling himself to stay.

A contradiction. Like gravity itself.

She looked around the room, searching for something to reconcile it. This was her last shot. Tom would never let her in here again.

"Come on, Dad," she pleaded. "Is there something else here?"

Cooper looked up from the pattern he was tracing.

"Don't you see, Tars?" he said. "I brought *myself* here. We're here to communicate with the three-dimensional world. We're the bridge."

He moved along to another version of the room. Murph was there, jumping up from the bed, grabbing the watch from where she had thrown it, running out the door…

* ✳ *

Murph reached into the box and picked up the watch, thinking about the little moment of hope, the little experiment she and her father were going to do together, until she realized just how long he was going to be gone, that he didn't even know if he was coming back. And then she had thrown it, rejected him and his damn attempt at "making things right."

Then she had picked it up again. And kept it. And waited. And he hadn't returned. They had never been able to compare them.

She put it on the bookshelf.

The second hand twitched.

Cooper pushed himself along the lines of the books, following their positions in time.

"I thought they chose me," Cooper said. "They never chose me. They chose Murph."

"For what?" Tars asked.

"To save the world!" Cooper replied.

He watched ten-year-old Murph come back into the room, crying her eyes out, holding the timepiece. It was hard to watch, but he did.

After a moment she put the watch on a shelf.

Murph sighed and put the box on the shelf. If there had ever been anything else here, it was gone now. She had to salvage what she could. And right now that meant saving Lois and Coop.

Cooper was "moving" fast now, following the room through space-time. Watching it go from being Murph's bedroom, to abandoned, to glimpses of what might be a little boy, although he never got a clear view.

""They'd have access to infinite time, infinite space," he told Tars, gesturing all around him. "But no way to find what they need. But I can find Murph and find a way to tell her—like I found this moment..."

"How?" Tars asked.

"Love, Tars," he said. "Love, just like Brand said. That's how we find things here." Love, like gravity, which could move across time and dimensions.

Brand had been spot on.

"So what are we to do?" Tars asked.

Cooper looked down the time dimension. The books? No, and not the lander. But the watch, on the shelf, as far as he could see...

"The watch," he realized. "That's it. She'll come back for it."

"How do you know?" Tars asked.

And again he felt the certainty, a pull as strong as a black hole. Stronger—it was like the pull that had brought him here. That would bring Murph back, too.

"Because I gave it to her," he said, excitement building. He scrutinized the watch for a moment. It would have to be simple, binary, or...

He had it.

"We use the second hand," he told Tars. "Translate the data into Morse, and feed it to me."

He grabbed the timeline that connected to the second hand in all of its iterations, and as the data came in he tugged it in time, long and short—dots and dashes.

"What if she never came back for it?" Tars asked.

"She will," he insisted, as the second hand began flicking back and forth. "She will. I can feel it..."

* ❄ *

Murph was turning to leave when Getty shouted—near hysterically—that Tom was coming. But still something held her. She went back to the box, knowing what she was going for, and pulled out the watch. Feeling it, then seeing it.

"Murph?" Getty yelled. "Murph!"

When she came tearing out of the house, Getty was holding a tire iron, watching an angry Tom climb from the truck, black with soot. Lois and Coop were watching, too, fearful looks on their faces.

But Murph ran straight for her brother.

"Tom," she said. "He came back... he came back."

Tom's fierce expression tempered a bit toward puzzlement.

"Who?" he asked, gruffly, confusion wrestling with anger in his voice.

"Dad," she told him. "It was him. He's going to save us."

Triumphantly she held up the watch—and its weirdly flickering second hand.

Murph looked at the equations she had just written, then back to the watch. She stood, gathering the pages, and hurried through the halls. In her haste she bumped into someone, and was absently aware that it was Getty, but she didn't slow her pace.

She remembered her first time here, with her dad, how terrifying it had been, followed quickly by awe-inspiring. Now, after all these years, it was home.

She reached the launch bay, the gigantic cylindrical space station that had never been intended to fly, had been nothing more than busy work to keep everyone who knew the truth from curling up into a ball and staying that way.

She remembered the pride Professor Brand had showed in the thing, even though he believed it would never function.

She walked up to the railing, marveling at it, at the thousands of workers who were still on the job. Getty stepped up beside her, having followed, and he wore a curious look on his face.

Then she turned back to the enormous hollow, and shouted at the top of her lungs.

"*Eu-RE-ka!*"

She turned her grin on Getty.

"Well, it's traditional," she said. Then she threw her papers over the railing.

"Eureka!" she repeated, as the papers fluttered down and workers looked curiously at her.

Then she planted a kiss right on the lips of a very surprised and confused Dr. Getty.

Cooper gazed along the worldline of the watch, saw that it seemed to branch out infinitely.

"Did it work?" he asked Tars.

"I think it might have," Tars replied.

"Why?" Cooper said, hopefully.

"Because the bulk beings are closing the tesseract," Tars replied.

Cooper gazed again off into the distance and saw that something, at least, was happening. The lines were becoming sheets, becoming bulks, as the three-dimensional representation created for his only-human brain unraveled and returned to its full five-dimensional reality. It was like the universe was collapsing in on him, which he supposed in a sense it was.

"You don't get it yet, Tars?" Cooper asked. "'They' aren't *beings*—they're *us*. Trying to help, just like I tried to help Murph…"

"People didn't build this tesseract," Tars said.

"Not yet," Cooper replied. "But one day. Not you and I, but people—people who've evolved beyond the four dimensions that we know."

As the expansion back into five dimensions came upon him, Cooper thought of Murph, and Tom—and hoped he had saved them. He thought he had, or at least played a part. There wasn't much more that he could ask.

"What happens now?" he wondered aloud.

But then he was swept away, as if by a massive wave, like the Ranger back on Miller's world. But that wave had only lifted and dropped him. No, this was more like a fast-moving river.

Or a riptide.

In the current, and beyond it, he saw stars and planets being born, dying, decaying into particles, then being born again, faster and faster—through space-time, above space-time, a piece of paper bending, a pen poking a hole through it…

Where was he going now? He was done, wasn't he? He'd accomplished what he was meant to do—it was up to Murph now. And Brand.

He wondered where Brand was, how she was doing. He wished he could explain to her why he'd had to leave her alone.

Ahead he saw a glassy, golden distortion, and in it the *Endurance*, and for a split second he thought his wish had brought him to her—but then he saw that this *Endurance* was like new, undamaged, just entering the wormhole. He drifted through the bulkhead and saw Brand and Romilly there, both strapped in.

Brand, he thought, reaching toward her. In a way, he *had* gotten his wish. Could he communicate with her? Probably not, or at least nothing important, since this was the past, and she hadn't known that any of this was going to happen.

To his surprise, she saw him. She reached her hand up to his, and he realized there *was* something he could communicate. Something that maybe was important. So he reached back, hoping to feel the warmth of her hand, give it an affectionate squeeze. But when their fingers came together they mingled, distorting each other but not really touching. A quiet moment in the chaos.

He watched her face, the wonder on it.

Then, abruptly, he was swept on. The sulfurous orb of Saturn suddenly loomed immense in his vision...

Then quiet.

THIRTY-FIVE

Cooper opened his eyes to the crack of a baseball bat, a faint breeze and gauzy sunlight. He blinked, trying to get his bearings.

He was no longer in a spacesuit. He lay in bed, tucked into crisp white sheets. The bed was in a room, and the room had a window that looked, not into space—but into light. The view was obscured by net curtains, but he could hear children laughing beyond it.

"Mr. Cooper?" someone asked. "Mr. Cooper?"

He looked up and found a young man with a pronounced chin and green eyes staring down at him. At his side was a woman with black hair in a ponytail. He didn't know either of them, but as his brain picked up a little speed he saw that they were dressed in medical clothing—and he realized the bed was a hospital bed.

He sat up, trying to remember. He had seen Brand, and then had the stuffing knocked out of him. And Saturn...

He had been pitched back into the space around Saturn, two years from Earth and any possible rescue.

So why wasn't he dead?

"Take it slow, sir," the man—a doctor, he saw now—

cautioned. "Remember you're no spring chicken anymore."
He smiled. "I gather you're—" The doctor referred to the
chart in his hand. "—one hundred and twenty four years
old."

Cooper didn't feel any older than when he'd left.

Time slippage, he thought.

"You were extremely lucky," he continued. "The Ranger
found you with only minutes left in your oxygen supply."

Rangers? Around Saturn? Why? Had there been
another expedition?

"Where am I?" he asked.

The doctor looked a little surprised, but then went to
the window and pulled back the curtains.

There was no sky, only the upper curve of a huge
cylinder, with upside-down houses, trees, fields, and pools.
Cooper followed what he could of the curve as it continued
down, realizing it went beneath him. And he knew had
seen this before, or something becoming this. Back at
NASA, in the mountain.

"Cooper Station," the doctor said. "Currently orbiting
Saturn."

Cooper struggled to get up and the nurse came to his
aid, helping him stand and walk slowly over to the window.
Outside, beneath the topsy-turvy sky, some kids were playing
baseball. As he watched, one swung like the devil and hit
a pop fly. He tracked it as it flew up, slowing, pausing—
then speeding up again as it crossed the station's axis and
continued on. The kids shouting warnings as the ball
shattered a skylight literally on the other side of the world.

"Nice of you to name the place after me," he said, as the
ball players laughed at their faux pas.

The nurse giggled. But when he looked, he could see
that it wasn't at the ball players, and the doctor was giving
her a look.

"What?" he asked.

"The station wasn't named after you, sir," the doctor said. "It was named after your daughter."

Cooper smiled at his mistake.

Of course it was.

"Although, she's always maintained how important you were," the man added quickly.

That brought up a question Cooper had to ask, but he wasn't at all sure he wanted to know the answer. If he was a hundred and twenty-four—if eighty-odd years had passed since he left Earth...

"Is she... still alive?" he asked.

"She'll be here in a couple of weeks," the doctor confirmed. "She's really far too old for a transfer from another station, but when she heard you'd been found—well, this is Murphy Cooper we're talking about."

"Yes," Cooper marveled, "it is."

"We'll have you checked out in a couple days," the doctor assured him. Then he and the nurse left Cooper alone.

Plan A, he mused, looking out at the fantastical station—Professor Brand's busy-work come to a fruition the old man had never himself believed would occur.

Freakin' plan A.

The administrator was very organized and very perky and—young. Thirty at most, with no hint of grey in his curly black hair.

"I'm sure you'll be excited to see what's in store," he told Cooper, leading him along a walkway inside of a hangar. "We've got a nice situation for you."

Cooper's gaze found a row of Rangers—not the ones he had flown but a new generation, even sleeker than before. Lovely to look at. How different were they, he wondered? He would love to climb into one, have a look at the controls. Were they propelled by some sort of gravity drive, as the station must be?

But his guide never even glanced at the handsome vessels. That wasn't where they were going.

"I actually did a paper on you in high school, sir," the fellow said. "I know all about your life on Earth…" They entered what would have been a quite ordinary town square had it not been in orbit around Saturn.

"So when I made my suggestion to Ms. Cooper, I was delighted to hear she thought it was perfect."

Cooper stopped, staring, at a farmhouse. No, scratch that. *The* farmhouse, his house, the same porch where he and Donald drank beers in the evening. The place where his kids were born, where Murph had turned her back to him.

But cleaner—it looked like they had painted it.

As he drew nearer, a monitor came to life, and an old man appeared on it.

"*May 14th*" the image said. "*Never forget. Clear as a bell. You'd never think…*"

Now Cooper saw another man's face, also old.

"*When the first of the real big ones rolled in,*" he said, "*I thought it was the end of the world.*"

"Of course," Cooper's guide said, "I didn't speak to her personally."

"*Sure, my dad was a farmer…*" the monitor continued, this time a woman's voice, quavering with age, but then they were in the house, the door closing off the narration. Another screen woke as they entered the kitchen, more old people talking about the dust, Cooper realized.

His house was now a museum exhibit.

"But she confirmed just how much you loved farming," the administrator finished, proudly.

"She did, huh?" Cooper said. Well, the least Murph deserved was a little joke at his expense. So he was going to live in a museum, and be its chief exhibit? Do a little hobby-farming to show the kids?

He noticed one thing in the house that didn't fit the pastoral scene in the least—a robot, quite familiar in form.

"Is that…?"

"The machine we found near Saturn when we found you, yes," the man confirmed. "Its power source was shot, but we could get you another, if you want to try and get it up and running again."

Cooper nodded.

"Please," he said.

That evening, Cooper went back to the hangar and watched the Rangers coming in from patrol, admiring their sleek lines, envying the pilots as they left their cockpits so the crews could wheel the craft into their resting places.

He wasn't altogether sure what brought him there. Only a few days ago—his time—he had been doing his level best to return to Earth and never see space—or a spaceship— ever again. Now—well, now he wasn't sure what he was supposed to do. That plan A had happened—that he had been able to help, and that Murph had managed to go from data to… *this*, was more than gratifying. It was more than he could ask. But there was a downside to being a hundred and twenty-four.

He would never see Tom again. His son had passed almost two decades ago, and his son Coop—Cooper's grandson—was biologically old enough to be *his* father. Almost everyone he knew was dead—except Murph.

As for Murph—he didn't know how that was going to go. For him, less than a year had passed since they sat together on her bed. For her, however, it had been a lifetime. He had been gone for most of her life. How did he apologize for that?

Sighing, he made his way back to the transplanted farmhouse, but he didn't hurry. Instead he took in the strange sights of Cooper Station.

Like the *Endurance*, the huge cylinder spun on its axis. The opening through which his ship had lifted off, so long ago, was essentially the station's North Pole. It was also the sun. The mirrors he remembered from the days when this place was a launch chamber—the ones that reflected sunlight down its vast shaft—had been replaced by *really* enormous mirrors, large enough to focus the light of Saturn's faint sun, yielding enough to illuminate the interior of Cooper Station. Computers kept them tracked and focused, and at dusk folded them up to simulate Earth's sleep cycle, or at least something like it.

Edmunds' world didn't have the same length day-and-night cycles as Earth, and since the eventual goal was to live there, Cooper Station—and her sister stations—were gradually modifying the length of each day. The human circadian rhythm had been the same for millions of years, and asking a body to change too quickly was generally considered to be a bad idea.

He wondered how Brand was doing with that. How she was doing, period. Had she made it? The time dilation had been the same for them. As he popped out into space near Saturn, she was still on course to Edmunds' world. She was either there, or would be soon. But when he considered everything she would have to accomplish, and all on her own, just to *reach* Edmunds' World—the course corrections, placing the *Endurance* into a stable orbit. Loading the population bomb onto the lander—along with anything else she would ever need, since there wasn't enough fuel to go back up once the lander had descended.

Taking the lander down would present its own set of problems. What if the atmosphere was unstable? The other planets had thrown them some freakin' hard curve balls. Even if the little red dot was habitable, who was to say it didn't have its own surprises?

And then, after all of that, she would have to build a camp, a home for the children to come.

Of course, she wasn't entirely alone. She had Case, and there was the long shot that Edmunds was still alive.

He tried to imagine the reunion, but found he didn't want to think about it. No doubt "Wolf" was a good guy, and he hoped for Brand's sake that he was still alive.

He really did.

But he didn't want to think about it too much.

Maybe they had already sent somebody to help her. Any of the Rangers was capable of making the trip, what with the wormhole still sitting right where it had been. He resolved to bring it up next time he saw the administrator. Wolf or no Wolf, Brand would need help.

When he returned to the farmhouse, he found that a new power supply had been brought, as promised, and so he began the work of bringing Tars back to life.

"Settings," Tars said. "General settings, security setting—"

"Honesty," Cooper said. "New level setting. Ninety-five percent."

"Confirmed," Tars replied. "Additional customization?"

"Yes," Cooper said. "Humor seventy-five percent. Wait... sixty percent."

"This place," Tars said. "Is this what your life on Earth was like?"

"Well, it was never this clean," Cooper said, glancing around the immaculate house—then beyond, through the windows at the houses and trees—which, their spatial orientation aside—represented a simulacrum of Earth.

"I'm not sure I like this pretending we're back where we came from," he murmured.

A nurse was waiting for Cooper as he nervously entered the hospital waiting room. He wasn't sure what to expect, wasn't even sure what he felt.

"Is she...?" He left it hanging, in a way not sure what the question really was.

"The family is all in there," the nurse told him.

"The family?" he asked.

"They all came to see her," she replied. "She's been in cryosleep for almost two years."

She indicated the door and, taking a deep breath, Cooper eased it open. No dresser this time. No chair.

She was there, on the bed, surrounded by people he didn't know, but many of them had little bits and pieces of Murph in their faces. Children, grandchildren, babies...

And Murph.

The family parted for him as he approached. Some of them were smiling, others looked curious, even puzzled. One little boy hid behind his mother's knee.

She looked very old, and very frail, but in her eyes he could see his daughter, the little girl with the flaming hair, the beautiful woman berating him over the comm. Murph, in all of her seasons.

Tears were in those eyes, but her face was joyful. She reached for him.

"Murph," he said, his throat constricting.

"Dad," she whispered. She nodded to the others,

and they quietly backed away.

"You told them I like farming," he said, shooting her a look.

She smiled that same mischievous smile she'd had when he caught her hiding in the truck. For a moment he just reveled in it.

"Murph," he said after a time. "It was me. I was your ghost."

"I know," she said, lifting her wrist, showing him the watch.

"People cidn't believe me," she continued. "They thought I'd done it all myself." She tapped the timepiece. "But I knew who it was..."

He regarded her—amazed, proud, happy, broken-hearted, all at the same time.

"A father looks in his child's eyes," Cooper said, "and thinks—maybe it's them—maybe my child will save the world."

Murph smiled.

"And everyone," she continued, "once a child, wants to look into their dad's eyes and know he saw. But usually, by then, the father is gone." She gripped his hand a little tighter. "Nobody believed me, but I knew you'd come back."

"How?" Cooper asked.

"Because my dad promised me," she replied.

Cooper felt tears rolling down his face.

"I'm here now," he said, seeing again how feeble, how tiny she looked. "I'm here for you Murph."

But Murph shook her head.

"No parent should ever have to watch their child die," she said. "My kids are here for me now. Go."

"Where?" he asked. Where in this world did he even belong? In that farmhouse?

"It's so obvious," Murph sighed.

And she told him.

When she finished talking, a few moments later, the family came back to her, attracted to her as if by gravity. He saw the love they had for her, and she for them. And even though they were also his family, it was as if he was watching from another dimension—as if he was once again Murph's ghost.

He left, but her words stayed with him.

"*It's so obvious,*" she'd said. "*Brand. She's out there.*"

EPILOGUE

Amelia watched, weeping, as Case excavated Wolf's pod, buried beneath a massive rock fall. Only the robot and the desert witnessed her grief.

Her gaze wandered over the rest—the pale gray sand and wind-hewn rocks where Edmunds had spent his final days. He had been in cryosleep when it happened, waiting for a rescue that would come years too late.

Cooper waited anxiously, watching the hangar door as the last of the mechanics left and locked up. He waited a few minutes, then crept near.

A moment later the door opened, and he was grinning at Tars.

"Setting up camp..."

Amelia knelt in front of the little cross and hung Wolf's name plate from it.

The first to die here, she thought, *but not the last.*

She reached up and broke the seal on her helmet. She

removed it and felt the cool air on her face. She took a slow, deep breath.

"Alone in a strange galaxy…"

Cooper pointed at one of the Rangers. Tars moved over to it and began working the hatch mechanism while Cooper kept a nervous eye out.

Amelia took a second breath, and a third. Her nose felt very dry, and she smelled something like salt and crushed pine needles.

"Maybe, right now, she's settling in for a long nap."

Tars beside him, Cooper strapped into the pilot seat, studying the controls. The robot ran a sequence as the hangar door opened to the familiar star-fretted darkness of space.

Cooper grinned. *Tomorrow, everyone's in for a little surprise.*

Still breathing, Amelia set her helmet aside and watched the unfamiliar, beautiful sunset.

"By the light of our new sun…"

She turned from the fading star and went back to camp. There was a lot to do, and she was the only one to do it. But she felt, somehow, it was going to be okay.

"In our new home."

ACKNOWLEDGMENTS

Thanks to Christopher and Jonathan Nolan for a fantastic screenplay.

Special thanks to Emma Thomas, Shane Thompson, Isabella Hyams, Kip Thorne, Jill Benscoter, Andy Thompson, and Josh Anderson at Warner Bros. for seeing that I got everything I needed to write this book. Thanks to Steve Saffel for suggesting this project to me—and as always, for deft editing. At Titan books I would also like to thank Nick Landau, Vivian Cheung, Katy Wild, Cath Trechman, Alice Nightingale, Tim Whale, Chris McLane, Sam Bonner, Owen Vanspall, Emma Smith, Julia Lloyd, Ella Bowman, and Katharine Carroll.

ABOUT THE AUTHOR

Greg Keyes was born John Gregory Keyes in 1963, in Meridian Mississippi to Nancy Joyce Ridout and John Howard Keyes. His mother was an artist, and his father worked in college administration. When he was seven, his family spent a year living in Many Farms Arizona, on the Navajo Reservation, where his father was business manager of the Navajo Community College. Many of the ideas and interests which led Greg to become a writer and informed his work were formed in that very important year. After another year or so in Flagstaff, the family returned to Bailey, Mississippi, where he and his brother Tim finished their public education and moved on to college. Greg received a B.A. in Anthropology from Mississippi State University, and afterwards worked briefly as a contract archaeologist. In 1987 he married Dorothy Lanelle Webb (Nell) and the two moved to Athens, Georgia, where Nell pursued a degree in art while Greg ironed newspapers for a living. During this time, Greg wrote several unpublished manuscripts before writing *The Waterborn*, his first published novel, followed by a string of original and licensed books over the following decade-and-a-half. Also during this time, Greg earned a Masters in Anthropology from the University of Georgia and completed the coursework and proposal for a Ph.D., which thus far remains A.B.D. Greg moved to Seattle for a few years where Nell earned her M.F.A. from the University of Washington, following which the couple moved to Savannah, Georgia. In 2005 the couple had a son, Archer, and in 2008 a daughter, Nellah. Greg continues to live with his family in Savannah, where he enjoys cooking, fencing, and raising his children.

Interstellar is his twenty-first published novel.

Did you enjoy this book? We love to hear from our readers.
Please email us at readerfeedback@titanemail.com or write to us at
Reader Feedback at the above address.

To receive advance information, news, competitions, and exclusive
offers online, please sign up for the Titan newsletter on our website

TITANBOOKS.COM